GREAT TEXAS
CHRISTMAS LEGENDS

by
Zeno Zeplin

Illustrated by
Judy Jones

NEL-MAR
Publishing

Second Edition
August 1987

Copyright 1987
by Nelson Eberspacher
All rights reserved.

Published by
Nel-Mar Publishing
HC-2, Box 267-C
Canyon Lake, Texas 78133-2705

Printed in the United States

Library of Congress Cataloging-in-Publication Data

Zeplin, Zeno, 1925-
   Great Texas Christmas Legends.

   Contents: The Elf's Cap — The Charge of the Elf's
Brigade — Whee-Whoo The Whistle — [etc.]
   1. Tales—Texas. [1. Folklore—Texas. 2. Christmas—
Folklore]   I. Title.
PZ8.1.Z44Gr   1987   398.2'09764   87-7675

ISBN 0-9615760-3-0

INTRODUCTION

Christmas is this world's most joyous celebration, for it brings the greatest promise of hope, love and peace, and a magnificent offer of redemption. The seasonal rituals and symbols we share bring all Christians together in the exultation of their common faith. Many customs express both basic theology and simple manifestations of our hearts' abundance in the comfort of believing. In several lands, for those too young to understand the deity of Christ and his covenant of salvation, a legendary, loving character has been created to reward children for being faithful and "good" at Christmas.

In 1822, Dr. Clement Moore "Americanized" those legends into his famous poem, *The Night Before Christmas,* and old Santa Claus has worked his wonders at Christmas ever since. All of Santa's origins have given him and the Christmas celebration a northern aura involving snow, sleighbells, fireplaces and such. To so many in warmer climes our Yuletide music and literature seriously lack a dimension that reaches into the South and West. Others see a pagan or irreverent essence in Santa, even though he was born of Christmas and serves no other motive. To these two wants we set our purpose in narrating these legends.

Texas is both Southern and Western, and its history and mystique provide a splendid heritage that seeds these stories.

DEDICATION

At Christmas we are all children.
We dedicate these legends to that
child in everyone who remembers
the joy of the age of wonder when
faith, love and imagination abound.

TABLE OF CONTENTS

The Elf's Cap

This morning in late December, 1883, found Galveston a bustling seaport and popular resort city. Tall-masted sailing ships and side-wheel steamers lined the docks, while others, with sails furled and boilers cold, rested quietly like sleeping giants out in the bay.

Along the busy waterfront, the routine quickened. Scurrying feet, tense voices and fading light forecast an intrusion suddenly present in the crisp snap of lightning and roll of thunder. A day that had begun bright with promise of pleasant working conditions and good fishing was quickly spoiled. The threatening sky, damp chill air and spattering rain drops sent everyone skittering for the shelter of a large wharf building on Galveston's commercial street, The Strand.

George P. Stone stood in a big door of the building facing the dock, hands on his hips, staring angrily out across the bay. An impatient man who hated interruptions, he had no sympathy for those who tolerated them. The scowl on his face reflected his displeasure. Lawyer Stone, known for his gruff, no-nonsense attitude, was by reputation tough and expensive. His surly demeanor and abrupt way of talking had gained him the dubious title of "Grumpy" Stone. His bushy hair, sturdy build, gray sideburns and thick black eyebrows made him look as formidable as he sounded.

In another door of the same building, perhaps thirty feet away, stood Thomas O'Duffy Hollyhan, as much an imp as the middle-aged man he was. He leaned against the door jamb, smiling, as he too gazed out across the bay. Also a local lawyer, Duffy, unlike Stone, was known for his relaxed, easy manner, countless friends, modest practice and entertaining guitar. He had a way of talking that could charm the devil out of his pitchfork or an eagle from the sky.

A small boat bumped against the dock. A distinguished looking old gentleman stowed his oars and fishing pole, tied off to a piling, and climbed out. Quickly, he made his way into the warehouse. Once inside, he wiped his face with his handkerchief, shook the rain water off his hat and began to clean his pipe.

"Why, Judge Whitlock," called Duffy Hollyhan. "Haven't seen you since the redfish run last year. How ya doing, Sir?"

"Well, hello, Duffy. I'm fine, and you're looking good."

"Thanks, Judge, you know just being here keeps me OK."

"Fishing is good, Duffy, maybe better even than last year. You catching any?"

"Yep, all I can eat, and some for my friends."

"Let's go over to Offats Bayou early in the morning."

"You're on, Judge. Meet you at my boat at daylight

and I'll have the bait."

"That's great, Duffy, I'll bring the lunch. Hey! Look, isn't that George Stone over there?"

"Looks like him, Judge."

"That you, George?" called the judge.

George Stone turned toward the two men approaching him.

"Well, who?—yeah! Judge Whitlock, haven't seen you in four or five years now. How are you, Sir?"

"Never better, George. I've retired and become addicted to fishing; right now the fishing is good. How are you?"

"Hrumph," complained Stone. "Lousy day. Hooked two big ones and lost 'em. Now this blasted rain ran me out of the bay while the fish are still biting."

"George, you remember Duffy Hollyhan here?"

"Yes, I'll never forget the likes of him."

Duffy grinned. "Might as well relax, Stone. It'll take a while for this cloud to blow over."

"Relax! Relax, indeed! I came here to catch fish," roared Stone.

"George, you're as grumpy as ever. I'd hoped you would have mellowed with age," chuckled the judge.

"Yeah, Judge, but if I was as mellow and relaxed as Hollyhan here, I'd be in the poorhouse and some of my clients would be in jail."

Duffy and Judge Whitlock laughed at Grumpy Stone's attitude. That seemed to irritate him all the more.

The rain increased steadily. Passengers disembarking from the Morgan Line, sailors, longshoremen, and other people off Central Wharf and The Strand began to collect in the big, dry warehouse to wait out the rain.

Grumpy Stone ranted about the rain, his fish that got away, and the noise some of the children were making. He continued until everyone in the building felt disgusted with his loud grumblings.

Duffy went over to quiet the youngsters. They asked him to play his guitar; so he sang several Christmas songs, some learned from foreign sailors and others all his own. The music attracted more people, and a crowd began to gather around him. As Duffy finished a song, he reached for a long red-and-white cap from Suzie Clark's curly head and took a tiny bell from the collar on Jimmy Thornton's dog. He tied the little bell to the topknot of the cap.

"You see, kids, anyone might wear a long red-and-white cap, but if you put a jinglebell on the topknot, it means you love Jesus and believe in Santa Claus. Now let me tell you about that jolly old elf."

As Duffy finished a song about Santa Claus, Jimmy Thornton looked puzzled. "Mr. Hollyhan, is Santa Claus real?"

"Why absolutely! There is no doubt about it."

Grumpy Stone jumped as if he'd sat on a tack and yelled at Duffy. "That's just your style, Hollyhan, feeding that kind of nonsense to the children. It's sentimental fools like you that spread such hogwash."

Duffy's expression changed to anger. Slowly he turned to face Stone. "Mr. Stone, that is an insult. It belittles my character, and slanders my professional abilities right here before my friends and clients. That is malicious and unethical, and even more grievous, it shows your gross ignorance by denying the very existence of Santa Claus."

Stone laughed with a great guffaw. "Fools like you and your Santa Claus should be exposed in court for the frauds you are, and silenced once and for all by court order."

Duffy jerked the stocking cap from his head and shook it in Stone's face. "So," he exclaimed sternly, "then I assume you believe you could prove to a jury that Santa Claus is not real."

"Any time, Hollyhan, any time," replied Stone, smugly.

"All right, Mr. Stone, let's see you prove Santa Claus is not real, right here, right now," challenged Duffy.

Placing his guitar against a cotton bale, Duffy went over to Judge Whitlock. After a short whispered conversation, the judge nodded in agreement, and Duffy turned to Stone.

"Mr. Stone, the Honorable Judge Whitlock has agreed to hold a simulated court right here and now in the interest of justice. As I see it, you must agree or admit to all these good folks that you are a loudmouth and a coward."

An ominous rumble rose from people nearby who witnessed Duffy's challenge. A ruddy-faced longshoreman yelled, "Yeah, big shot, let's see you prove it now."

"Come on, Stone, prove it," dared another.

"I would be most happy to oblige all of you," said Lawyer Stone, bowing to the crowd. "But I see no need to pursue this matter today. Perhaps later."

"No, Stone, we will do it now," demanded Duffy sternly. "It's the Christmas season, and with such blasphemous statements about Santa Claus from a man of your reputation, immediate action is mandatory. You have insinuated in public that Santa Claus is not real. I demand justice now."

Again the crowd rose in a chorus of voices demanding Stone prove it now or admit he was totally wrong about the old elf.

George Stone felt cornered and threatened by the

crowd. He had to respond.

"Insinuated my foot!" he exploded. "I'll make it plainer than that, you nin-com-poop. I'll put it in language even you can understand. THERE IS NO SANTA CLAUS. Now, what do you say to that?"

"Well, that was short, simple and right to the point, I think I like it that way."

"Hollyhan, you half-wit, just what is this court supposed to decide?"

"That is simple, Mr. Stone. It will decide which one of us is right about Santa Claus."

"So what?" Stone's expression reflected his disgust and annoyance.

"Well, as you say, I'll just put that in language even you can understand, Stone. One of us will end up a long-eared donkey. How is that?" challenged Duffy.

"Well, now," mused Stone, looking suddenly thoughtful. "That is interesting. Yes, yes, I like the prospect." Stone rose, paced back and forth, stroking his chin. "There might be a little amusement in this lousy day yet."

He strutted over to the judge, who sat puffing his pipe and smiling. "Court rules for this little game, Your Honor?"

"Gentlemen," said the judge, "as moderator for this debate, I propose we follow general court procedure, select a jury for a decision and end it all in time for dinner. Agreed?"

Duffy nodded. "Sounds good to me, Judge."

"Agreed," shouted Stone.

"Why not pick a jury right from this group?" Duffy queried.

Stone looked around. "Say, we do seem to have quite a crowd." For indeed, by this time, the rain, the

music, and the loud talk had drawn a number of people into the big warehouse.

"Mr. Hollyhan, would it be agreeable with you for the judge to take a list of volunteers for a jury?" asked Stone very formally.

"Agreed!" said Duffy.

The judge got up, borrowed paper and pencil from a tallyman. Climbing up on a bale of cotton, he asked for quiet while he organized the court. Longshoremen moved bales of cotton, planks, kegs, boxes and such to approximate a courtroom.

"I will need about two dozen volunteers for jury duty, and my only requirement is that you speak and understand English reasonably well." People raised their hands and moved forward to give the judge their names.

The list completed, he called the names one by one. Hollyhan and Stone asked each a few questions and made notes, then handed the Judge their selections. In a moment, he annoucnced the names of those chosen for the jury.

Judge Whitlock picked up a crating hammer and pounded on a board on top of the bale of cotton that was to serve as his bench. He studied the crowd a moment and cleared his throat. "This simulated court will come to order."

In a stern and serious voice, he said, "An age-old question, that at one time or another has been important to each of us, has today become a point of honor between these two astute counselors."

Grumpy Stone interrupted loudly. "Your Honor, I object to wasting a good adjective like 'astute' on this— this sentimental incompetent, Hollyhan."

"Overruled," the judge banged his hammer for silence, then continued, "Our purpose is to determine, by orderly court procedure, if Santa Claus is real. Mr. Stone and Mr. Hollyhan will please approach the bench."

The two attorneys went over to the judge. Following a low voiced, but heated discussion, both men nodded in agreement.

Judge Whitlock said, "Ladies and Gentlemen, the defendant today will be Santa Claus himself. Mr. Stone will act as the Prosecuting Attorney, who alleges Santa Claus is not real. Mr. Hollyhan will act as Counsel for the Defense. The jury will decide the ultimate verdict. This court will adjourn for one hour for lunch, and to allow the attorneys time to prepare."

The warehouse buzzed with excited voices as the judge left for lunch at the nearby Palmetto House Restaurant.

George Stone gave a boy money to fetch him some food while he talked to several sailors and made notes.

Duffy sent two kids to get his briefcase and newspaper from his office. Munching an apple retrieved from his coat pocket, he talked briefly to Captain Watt, Master of the barque, Elissa. He borrowed a chair from the tallyman's desk and placed it beside a big crate to serve as defense counsel's table. He stared thoughtfully at the long red-and-white cap, folded it reverently, and put it in his pocket.

Spying Sammy Martinez, Duffy snapped his fingers as a thought popped into his head. "Sammy," he said, "show me what you have in your pockets." Sammy produced a handful of assorted junk, and Duffy reached in. "May I borrow that silver dollar, Sammy?"

"But, Duffy, that is my lucky piece," protested Sammy.

"Don't worry, you'll get it back. OK?"

"Sure, Duffy."

When the kids arrived with the things from Duffy's office, he sat down and thumbed through the paper slowly, mumbling to himself now and then, even smiling occasionally. Taking some paper from his briefcase, he wrote a note and gave a boy a coin, saying, "Please take this to Mandy Scott."

Those who had lunches for work or fishing ate there in the warehouse. Others scampered out to get something to eat, but all returned, and it seemed others came also as the news got around. The warehouse was filling with people. Everyone found bales, barrels, and crates to sit on to witness the proceedings. No one noticed or cared when the rain stopped. The events happening now were more important than fishing or working on the docks.

Judge Whitlock returned, took his seat, and looked over the crowd thoughtfully. He gaveled the warehouse to silence and began to set the court in order. "Captain Watt, the Elissa is nearby, would you be so kind as to loan us your ship's Bible?"

"It would be an honor." He set off to fetch it.

"Captain Jordan, would you act as Bailiff for these proceedings?"

"Of course, Your Honor."

Tommy English, a young reporter for the *Galveston Daily News,* rushed up to Captain Jordan to ask him a question. As he made notes on a pad, the judge called to him, "The gentleman with the note pad will approach the bench." Tommy English stood dumbfounded a moment, then turned to the judge who asked, "Sir, are you a reporter?"

"Yes, Your Honor."

"Then be seated right there and record these proceedings for this court as well as for your paper."

"Oh, yes, Sir."

"We have a court reporter; now we need a marshall. Ah, Constable Burke, if anyone disturbs the order of this court, would you please remove him from this warehouse, er—courtroom?"

"Yes, Sir, Judge."

"Then, let us proceed." The judge seated the jury, instructed them to listen carefully and weigh the evidence and logic of each argument so they would reach a fair and just verdict. Then he asked both attorneys for opening statements.

Grumpy Stone stood up. "There is not one person in this warehouse—er—courtroom who is old enough to find his way home who does not understand that Santa Claus and all the stories about him are fairy tales," he began. "Now I will prove beyond a doubt that he has not, does not, and will not exist. And what's more, it has stopped raining, and we ought to stop listening to this babbling and get back to fishing."

Boos and cat-calls came from the crowd, and the judge gaveled for silence.

Duffy rose from his chair and said eloquently, "Gentlemen of the Jury, I will present undeniable evidence of who Santa is, that he is real and why he is real. Furthermore, I will prove that the apparent hardness of Mr. Stone's heart is only a reflection of his hard head and big mouth."

Stone bellowed. "What is this? The donkey kicks? Haw, haw."

Judge Whitlock pounded for order. "One more outbreak of remarks like that and I will adjourn this court."

"Sorry, Your Honor," apologized Stone.

"My apologies, Your Honor," said Duffy.

"This is indeed a serious matter and everyone in this courtroom will consider it so or out he goes. Is the defense ready?"

"Yes, Your Honor. If it pleases the Court this chair and Elf's Cap will serve to remind us who the defendant is and even where he is."

"Any objection from the prosecution?" asked the judge.

"I like that just fine, Your Honor."

"Then proceed with the prosecution, Mr. Stone."

Grumpy got up. "Thank you, Your Honor." He walked over to the empty chair, picked it up, held it over his head. "See, it is empty." While he was making a big show of this, Duffy calmly fitted the red-and-white stocking cap on his head. He turned his head quickly from side to side so the tiny bell would jingle. Stone set the chair down and stood looking disgustedly at Duffy's antics.

"Judge Whitlock, haw, haw! This—er—counselor is

wearing Santa Claus' cap. Perhaps he wants us to believe he is Santa Claus." Grumpy sat down still laughing to himself.

Hollyhan got up, still wearing the red-and-white cap. "Thank you, Mr. Stone. Let the record show that Mr. Stone referred to this as 'Santa Claus' cap', and that I am wearing it. Gentlemen of the Jury, the fact that Mr. Stone recognized Santa's cap is important, please remember that. I would like to submit for your further consideration that I am indeed wearing it, and equally important, anyone so inclined could wear it."

"Objection," shouted Stone.

"Overruled," said Judge Whitlock calmly, smiling.

"I would like to call a witness, Your Honor," Duffy said, as he removed the cap and walked around in the building, obviously studying the crowd for a moment.

Then he pointed, "That young lady with the pigtails and sparkling blue eyes."

"Objection," shouted Grumpy, "the testimony of a small child cannot be seriously considered in a court of law, Your Honor."

The judge looked thoughtful. There was a long silence.

"Your Honor," interrupted Duffy, "this case was brought about by Mr. Stone's charge that Santa Claus is 'just nonsense we feed to children', so I submit that the beliefs and opinions of children about Santa Claus are indeed important considerations."

"Objection overruled, Mr. Stone," said the judge as he banged his crating hammer on the board.

Duffy went back to the little girl. "Will you tell us what you know about Santa Claus, young lady?"

She looked at Duffy for a long moment, then up at her mother. Her mother said, "It's all right, Honey." The little girl nodded to Duffy.

He smiled, picked her up, and carried her to the witness chair by the judge's bench.

"I chose you because you are so neat and pretty. Now would you please tell us your name?"

"Sally."

"What is your whole name, Sally?"

"Sally Marie Brown, Sir."

"That is a pretty name, too. Now, Miss Sally Brown, would you tell me what this is?"

"The Bible," she said solemnly.

"What is it about?"

"God and Jesus, Sir."

"Your Honor, do you wish to swear in this witness?" asked Duffy.

"Please do, Captain Jordan."

Captain Jordan held the large black book toward Sally. "Miss Brown, will you put your hand on the Bible and tell us that you will only say what you really believe to be true?"

"Yes, Sir," replied Sally, as she put her hand on the Bible.

"Thank you, Sally," replied the captain.

"Now, Sally," said Duffy, "do you believe Santa Claus is real?"

"Yes, Sir." She nodded very seriously.

"Why?"

"Mamma and Papa told me so, and Grandpa and Luke—Luke is my big brother—and Mr. Smithers at the store."

"Is there any other reason you believe Santa Claus is real?"

"Well, he brought me a doll last Christmas."

"How did you know it came from Santa?"

"His picture was on the tag, and Luke read it to me. It said 'To Sally, From Santa.' "

"When did you first learn about Santa, Sally?"

"Oh, I don't remember." She paused thoughtfully. "I think I've just known forever."

The crowd cheered and clapped approvingly. The judge pounded for order.

"Do you know a story that tells about Santa?"

"Oh, yes, Sir," she said excitedly. " 'Twas the night before Christmas and all through the house, nobody was awake, not even a mouse and—and—.' " She giggled, "I forgot how it goes, but it is about Santa and Dancer and Prancer and snow and, and all about a Happy Christmas."

"Perhaps I have the poem right here. Let me read it, and you tell me if it is the one you remember, OK?"

"Objection," shouted Grumpy. "What has that got to do with that empty chair?"

"Overruled, Mr. Stone. The jury needs to know the origin of stories about Santa Claus."

"Thank you, Your Honor." Duffy took a Christmas card from his briefcase and very eloquently read the well-known Christmas poem aloud.

"Hrumph," muttered Grumpy Stone, in loud disgust.

"Was that the right story, Sally?"

"Yes, Sir." Sally giggled.

"Sally, you have told us you believe Santa is real and why you believe it. Now Santa bringing you toys makes Christmas a wonderful time. Is there something else perhaps more important about Christmas?"

"Oh, yes, Sir." She stood up, pigtails bouncing, and clapped her hands. "It's Baby Jesus' Birthday."

"Wonderful. You are a very smart young lady. I have another question, Sally. Tell us why you think Santa Claus isn't here to sit in that chair today."

"That's easy. He is home getting all his toys ready to bring in this many days." She held up three fingers.

"Thank you, Sally Brown. You are as smart as you are pretty. Now, one last question. What do children do for Santa? He must expect something for all the gifts he delivers at Christmas."

Sally frowned thoughtfully for a moment, then beamed.

"We just love him."

"Gentlemen of the Jury," said Duffy, "Mr. Stone offered the empty chair as proof that Santa Claus is not real. Even this child knows Santa is too far away and too busy preparing for the world's greatest Birthday Party, only three days away (Duffy held up three fingers as Sally had done) to be here right now. Your witness, Mr. Stone."

Grumpy Stone jumped to his feet. "Miss Brown, tell me the honest truth now. Have you ever talked to or even seen the real, er, ah, what you knew to be the real Santa Claus?"

"Oh, yes, Sir."

"Where?"

"At our church last year, and I will see him again tonight."

"What makes you think he is or was the real Santa Claus?"

"He was fat and happy and nice, and he promised me a doll and he brought it to me."

"Didn't you ask for more than a doll?"

"Yes, Sir, and Santa Claus said I shouldn't ask for so many things because there were lots of other children who wanted toys too, so I knew he was real."

"Why would that make him real?"

" 'Cause that is what my father said too."

There were nods and mumbles of approval from the crowd.

"Why did you ask for a doll, Sally?"

"So I could love it like Mary and Joseph loved Baby Jesus. You sure do ask silly questions, Mr. Stone. Didn't your mama and papa ever tell you about Christmas?"

The crowd broke into cheers and applause. Judge Whitlock pounded to silence the gales of laughter.

Grumpy was embarrassed. "No further questions, Your Honor."

Captain Jordan helped Sally down.

"Now I want to call a witness, Your Honor," said Stone. "I call Rolf Schmidt."

A weathered old sailor took the stand, and Captain

Jordan swore him in.

"Mr. Schmidt," said Stone. "You are familiar with the stories and legends of Santa Claus in this country?"

"Yes, Sir."

"Are you also familiar with similar stories in other countries, including your native Germany?"

"Yes, Sir."

"Tell me about some of them."

"In Germany, an old man called Pelze-Nicol is said to visit all good children at Christmas. In England, it is Father Christmas, and in Holland, it's Sinterklaas who adds much joy to the season. In other Christian countries there are similar Christmas stories."

"Do you believe Santa Claus or Father Christmas or Pelze-Nicol or any of the others are real?"

"No, Sir."

"And why not?"

"Well, Sir, they are wonderful Christmas legends, but their names are all different, and I have never met one that I knew to be real."

There were muffled groans from the crowd.

"Do you ever expect to meet a real one then?"

"No, Sir."

Again there were low sounds of disappointment.

"Thank you, Mr. Schmidt. Your witness, Mr. Hollyhan."

Duffy walked up to Rolf Schmidt, and looked at him quietly a moment. "Mr. Schmidt, are you Christian?"

"Oh, yes, Sir, I would find it fearful to sail the seas without faith in the Almighty."

"Mr. Schmidt, is Jesus called 'Jesus' in every language?"

"Why, no, Sir."

"Have you ever met a man that you knew to be the

-17-

real Jesus?"

"Of course not, Sir."

"Then am I to assume by the logic just presented by you that you do not really believe in Jesus and never expect to meet the real one?"

The crowd responded with a quiet murmur of approval of Hollyhan's question.

"Now, wait a minute here. I do believe in Jesus. I told you that."

"Yes, Mr. Schmidt, you did. My point is your logic for not believing in Santa Claus is rather inconsistent with your other beliefs, is it not?"

Rolf Schmidt held up his hands in despair.

"No further questions of this witness, Your Honor. Now I would like to call another witness, Captain Henry Watt, from the good ship, Elissa," said Duffy.

"Thank you, Mr. Schmidt," said Judge Whitlock as the witness stepped down. "Would you please take the stand, Captain Watt?"

Captain Watt stood up and strode majestically to the witness chair. His cap, pipe and long coat immediately set him apart as every bit the captain, an old salt with a distinctive beard and flashing eyes. "Aye, Sir, indeed I will." His booming voice reflected the commanding authority of a great ship's master.

Captain Jordan swore in Captain Watt.

"Captain, will you please tell the court in your own words what you have learned about Santa Claus?" asked Duffy.

"Aye, Mr. Hollyhan. Your Honor, may I stand up to talk? You see a captain doesn't sit much, so I think and talk better on my feet."

"Certainly you may, Captain."

Captain Watt paced a few steps each way, puffing his

pipe and looking thoughtfully at the jury. He stopped, tapped himself on the chest with his pipe stem. "I am Captain Henry Watt, and for forty-eight years I have sailed God's fabulous sea. I have known its beauty and its wrath, and it has taught me many wonderful things. As master of many fine ships, I have carried the people and the goods of every land to the ports of call of every nation in the world. Now as a ship's captain, I have made it my affair to know much about life's mysteries. I must know the sun, moon and stars, the trade winds, tides and ocean currents, the habits and names of fishes and birds, and most importantly, the languages and customs of men of all lands. Now in all the years of adventure I have enjoyed with people both bad and good from north, south, east, and west, there is one thing I have learned best, and that is this truth about Santa Claus."

He paused and pointed his pipe toward the jury to emphasize his words. "In those lands that fear God and love Jesus Christ and celebrate His Birth, there is a tenderness in the faces and philosophy of the people. There is more friendliness, honesty, trust, love and hope in the words and deeds of the people than in non-Christian lands. Without fail, in each Christian land, there are tales of one who brings joy to people at Christmas time."

The captain puffed his pipe and slowly began to pace again. "One strange thing about the one in all such tales is that he concerns himself in the main with children and asks naught for himself. So much joy is spread by him, or in his name, that I can only conclude that his actions proclaim the abundance of love in the hearts of those who perpetuate his fame. I see his treasure in his gifts to the young and the needy. I see him confirmed in the winks and twinkles of many an eye. And I hear his laughter in many voices that sing joy to mankind and praise to the Lord at Christmas time."

He paused to·puff his pipe. "You see, Mates, I believe in Santa Claus." He returned to the witness chair.

"Thank you, Captain," said Duffy. "Your witness, Mr. Stone."

Stone got up with a disgusted look and approached the captain. "Captain Watt, I heard all your eloquent words about the fine deeds supposedly done by Santa Claus, but you offered not one shred of evidence that he is real. Have you seen him?"

"No, Sir, but that is his way," said the captain, in matter-of-fact tones. He smiled and looked askance at Stone.

"Do you agree that every land has a different name for its Christmas hero?"

"Aye! that is true."

"Then why do you not find this inconsistency alone reason to doubt Santa Claus is real?" demanded Stone.

"Mr. Stone," replied the captain firmly, then pausing between statements for emphasis and effect. "You call me 'Captain Watt'. My son calls me 'Pop'. My mother calls me 'Hank'. My wife calls me 'Pokey' and sailors I have known have called me many names that I try to forget. No matter what I am called I am never unreal. I am always the same old me. So it is with Santa Claus. Don't you see, Mr. Stone?"

The crowd reacted with cheers and laughter.

The judge stifled a smile as he pounded for order.

"Hrumph," said Grumpy, disgustedly. "No more questions."

"Thank you, Captain Watt," said the judge. "You may step down."

"Your Honor," said Duffy, "I would like to call my next witness, Mr. Sammy Martinez."

Sammy took the stand and Captain Jordan swore him in.

Duffy walked up to Sammy and flipped him the silver dollar. "What is that, Sammy?"

"That is my lucky dollar."

"You are right, Sammy; it is a dollar. Everyone knows a dollar when he sees it." Duffy took the coin from Sammy and walked along in front of the jury, holding it for them to see. He gave the silver dollar back to Sammy, took out his wallet and handed Sammy a one-dollar bill. "What is that, Sammy?"

"That is a dollar."

"Well, now," mused Duffy. "Is this confusing?"

Stone jumped up. "Your Honor, lecturing us on money is ridiculous. We know what money is. I object to this waste of time. We are talking about Santa Claus."

"Counselor," admonished the judge sternly, "get to the point."

"Yes, Sir," replied Duffy. "My point is that the silver dollar is a real dollar, yet this paper dollar is a convenient substitute. One is just as useful as the other. Now, Gentlemen of the Jury, if you tried to carry a hundred silver dollars, real dollars, if you please, around with you, I dare say you would have trouble keeping your pants up. Ooops, sorry, Ladies."

The judge pounded for silence as the crowd howled with laughter. Even Grumpy Stone laughed.

"The point I want to make is that Santa would also find it difficult to make his Christmas rounds if it weren't for the help of some convenient substitutes who, like this dollar bill, get the job done just as well, or perhaps even better."

Chuckles, applause and even a hearty ho, ho, ho echoed the approval of the gallery.

Duffy went back to his table, picked up the newspaper and opened it. "This is the editorial page of today's paper."

Stone suddenly looked surprised. He snapped his fingers and smiled as if he had just caught the biggest fish in the bay. He waved to a boy nearby, gave him a coin, and whispered to him. The lad rushed out and hurried up The Strand.

Duffy continued, "Sammy, who is this?"

"Why, that is Uncle Sam."

Duffy passed in front of the jury, holding up the picture in the paper. "Now many nations are known by their king or queen or dictator. Here in America, we have no royalty. All we have is a symbol, a mythical old gent called Uncle Sam. He isn't flesh and blood, but he is real enough because he stands for all we hold dear. He represents the Constitution and the Bill of Rights and 'government of, by and for the people.' You might say he represents you and me and what we believe."

Laying aside the newspaper, Duffy picked up the red-and-white cap admiringly to focus the jury's attention on the old elf and continued, "Let me submit to you that Santa Claus symbolizes what you and I believe in also, and that is unselfishness and the joy of giving, which is in the best Christian teaching. Now, I also believe that old Santa's preoccupation with children is for a purpose. He is a beginning in understanding Jesus. Small children cannot understand or appreciate the miracle of Christ's birth or the implications of his offer of salvation. They can indeed understand the joy Santa Claus finds in making them happy while expecting nothing in return except that they love him."

Duffy paused a moment for the jury to absorb the logic of his statement. "Now, as children mature, these principles and logic learned early are, let's say, convertible. In time we come to understand that the greatest and most precious of all Christmas gifts is the promise of salvation through Jesus, who only expects us to accept Him and love Him. So we believe in Jesus and His promise of life everlasting. We believe in the principles of government represented by Uncle Sam. We believe in the do-it-yourself unselfishness and love that is represented by Santa Claus. You see, he is just as real as you and I, just as real as we want him to be."

The crowd responded with reverent oh's, ah's and amen's.

"Thank you, Sammy." Duffy went back to his seat.

"Any questions for this witness, Mr. Stone?"

"No, Your Honor. Well, so much for the sermon from the fountain of foolishness," scoffed Stone. "Let us get back to reality. I call Mr. David Jenkins as my next witness."

"Thank you, Mr. Martinez," said the judge as Sammy Martinez returned to his place in the crowd.

David C. Jenkins, editor of the *Galveston Daily News,* was entering the building accompanied by the boy Stone had sent for him. Mr. Jenkins, a wise-looking, gray-haired gentleman, had his sleeves rolled up, indicating the interruption from his day's work. He glanced quizzically about the crowded warehouse. "What is this all about?" His voice sounded puzzled.

"Mr. Jenkins, if you will come here I will explain this proceeding to you," said the judge.

While Judge Whitlock and George Stone explained how this all got started, and what was happening, Duffy just sat quietly thumbing through the paper. He folded it carefully to one certain page.

Dave Jenkins looked worried as he took the stand and the oath.

Stone approached him. "Mr. Jenkins, you are editor of the *Galveston Daily News,* is that correct?"

"Yes, that is right."

"You wrote an editorial in yesterday's paper about truth in reporting, truth in government and politics. I believe you said that truth is the foundation of our society, and without it there is no security for any of us. Our future would be without hope. Am I correct?"

Dave Jenkins was emphatic. He slapped his knee. "Yes, that is correct. I wrote it, and I believe that with all my heart and soul."

"Thank you, Mr. Jenkins. Now as a reporter with many years of experience, would you please tell us the simple truth? Is Santa Claus real?"

In the moment of silence, one could hear the seagulls' shrill cries far out in the bay.

Dave Jenkins rubbed his chin thoughtfully as he looked around the warehouse at the variety of faces waiting for his reply. With a sparkle in his eye, he said, "Mr. Stone, you want a simple, positive yes-or-no answer that would reflect personal knowledge of the old elf in the flesh or the absolute lack of it. Am I correct?"

"Dave, just say yes or no, please," begged Stone, with a pained look.

"You want a definite statement of fact, but the best I can offer is a personal opinion."

"Humbug, Dave, you're talking like a politician, not a reporter. Now let's have a straight answer," replied Grumpy.

"To be positive requires proof. We have all heard of Santa Claus, and I must say I have seen the results of his work. I have seen the joy and love in the eyes of needy children on Christmas morning holding a doll or pulling a red wagon. I have heard his 'ho, ho, ho!' echoed by unseen voices. I have shared the inner warmth of the unnamed giver who from his heart has said, 'It is from Santa Claus.' You see, when one can act like Santa Claus and share in the joy of giving, one has learned the real meaning of the First Christmas. Indeed, I have found the elf in self. Now that is the truth."

There was a stir of quiet appreciation of the editor's conclusion.

"Dave, you are an impossible witness," complained Stone.

"Mr. Stone," said Dave Jenkins apologetically, "I

have not been to the North Pole to check personally on the existence of Santa Claus or his workshops, sleigh and reindeer team. Without such proof, the existence of one jolly old elf in the flesh is, perhaps for some questionable."

"He is more than questionable," shouted Stone. "He is a myth, and you know it."

Exasperated, Grumpy silently paced back and forth in front of his witness. "No more questions. Your witness, Hollyhan."

Duffy walked up to Dave Jenkins, carrying the folded newspaper under his arm.

"Mr. Jenkins," he said admiringly, "in reference to your editorial about the value of truth, I have read your paper long enough to know that you believe in honesty and practice it. I recall another of your editorials one day last week about love and charity, and the opportunity one has when in a position to give. You said the true spirit of Christmas is not gifts, but faith, love and generosity that express the heart's abundance."

"Yes, I said that," said Jenkins proudly.

"I know you believe it because I have seen the results of the Christmas projects that you and many good folks have done every year. I have also seen the joy in your faces. Personally I believe it often quietly out-measures the glee of the receivers." Duffy winked at Dave Jenkins. "I'm sure old Santa is proud of you."

Grumpy Stone jumped up, waving his fists. "Objection, you're not here to praise the witness, Mr. Hollyhan," he shouted. "You are here to question him. Now ask him something useful."

The laughter from the crowd made Stone fume. Even Duffy and Dave Jenkins laughed at Grumpy's outburst.

"Sustained." The judge was obviously trying to keep

from laughing himself.

Duffy unfolded the newspaper. "Speaking of the truth, would you read the headline of this article on Page Two of today's paper?"

Dave Jenkins read it loud and clear, " 'SANTA CLAUS TO BE AT THE GARTEN VEREIN PAVILION TOMORROW, at 2:00 P.M.' "

"Now, read this one."

" 'SANTA TO VISIT CHILDREN AT THREE CHURCHES THIS WEEK.' "

"Now, this one under the picture of the parade."

" 'SANTA CLAUS AND THE MAYOR LEAD CHRISTMAS PARADE ON THE STRAND,' " read Jenkins.

"And here is his picture." Duffy held the paper for all to see.

Judge Whitlock pounded for order as the crowd cheered. The children were laughing and dancing and shouting, "See! see! there he is."

When order was restored, Duffy said, "No more questions, Mr. Jenkins, and thanks."

"Next witness, Mr. Stone?" asked the judge.

"No more witnesses." Stone waved his hand in disgust. "This has gotten impossible. The whole darned world is full of idiots, absolute imbeciles." He continued to wave his arms in gestures of despair.

"Do you have another witness, Mr. Hollyhan?" asked the judge.

"Yes, two, Your Honor. First, I would like to call Mrs. Mandy Scott."

George Stone's mouth opened. He jumped to his feet and looked for a moment as if he had seen a ghost. "Your Honor, I protest."

"On what grounds, Mr. Stone?"

"Well, ah, well, I don't know, but I don't like this," protested Stone. He wiped his hand over his face, clinched his fist, looked up and shook his head, and groaned. "Hollyhan, this is a dirty trick."

"Something inspired by a pompous loudmouth colleague, I assure you, Mr. Stone," said Duffy, sarcastically.

Judge Whitlock pounded for order and chided Duffy.

A smiling black woman took the stand and Captain Jordan swore her in.

"Mrs. Scott," said Duffy, "do you believe in Santa Claus?"

"Yes, I do."

"Do you know Mr. Stone, Mrs. Scott?"

"Yes, Suh, I shoah do."

"Where have you known him?" asked Duffy.

"He defended my son when he was arrested for stealing a horse and buggy."

"Was he successful in defending your son?"

"Oh, yes, Suh, he proved my boy didn't do it, and he got the real thief sent to jail."

Grumpy Stone jumped up. "Your Honor, this line of questioning has nothing to do with this case. I object."

"Mr. Hollyhan, show quickly that this line of questioning is relevant, or I will have to stop it."

"Yes, Your Honor, I will. Now, Mrs. Scott, as I recall your son's trial was long and difficult. I believe Mr. Stone did a very professional, even brilliant, job of investigation and defense."

"Oh, yes, Suh, he was just fantastic."

"Tell me, Mrs. Scott, was he as grumpy then as he is today?" asked Duffy, snickering.

"Objection, objection," shouted Stone, immediately. The audience howled and the judge pounded for silence.

"Sustained," shouted the judge. "Cut that out, Holly-han."

"Yes, Sir, Your Honor," said Duffy apologetically. "I believe he owed me one or two for the names he has called me today."

"Hrrumph," grumbled Stone, looking disgusted.

"Mrs. Scott, one would expect the cost of Mr. Stone's legal services in that case to be very high. How did you afford it?"

"Well, he sent me a bill all right."

The warehouse was quiet again as everyone strained to hear.

"Is this the bill he sent you?" Duffy handed her a slip of paper.

"It shoah is."

"Objection, objection." Stone rushed up to the judge again waving his arms pleadingly.

"Let me see that," demanded Judge Whitlock.

Duffy handed him the paper. The judge's eyes popped open wide, as he struggled to compose himself. "This is relevant, Mr. Stone. Objection overruled."

"As I recall your son's trial was concluded in December. Mrs. Scott, would you tell us the date on this bill?"

"December twenty-first."

"Now, would you tell us what it says on this bill, please?"

"Yes, Suh, it says, 'Merry Christmas to you and your son, Mrs. Scott. Santa Claus came in this morning and paid your bill in full. Signed—G.P. Stone.' "

There was a moment of silence. People began to stand and applaud. Mrs. Scott wiped the tears from her eyes.

Grumpy Stone just sat, shoulders sagging, with his

face held in his hands.

When quiet was restored, Duffy continued, "Would you tell us what else is on the bill, please, Mrs. Scott?"

Again there was attentive silence. She wiped the happy tears from her eyes again. " 'P.S. There is a tax, however, that I must insist be paid, and that is one of your most delicious apple pies.' "

The silence was broken only by a few ah's and oh's. Several were seen wiping away a tear.

"What was the significance of the pie, Mrs. Scott?" asked Duffy.

"Well, Mr. Stone came to my house quite often, working on the case, and he just loved my apple pie."

"Did you pay the tax, Mrs. Scott?"

"Oh, land yes. My heart was so full of joy and relief and appreciation for Mr. Stone, I baked him a pie big as a wagon wheel."

Shouts, cheers and applause filled the big warehouse.

"Thank you, and God bless you, Mrs. Scott. Your witness, Mr. Stone."

Grumpy never looked up. "No questions."

"Thank you, Mrs. Scott. You may step down," said the judge.

Applause followed Mandy Scott as she walked away from the witness chair.

"Merry Christmas, Mandy," said Duffy.

"Do you have another witness?" asked the judge.

"Yes, Your Honor, I would like to call Mr. George P. Stone."

There was a moment of stunned silence.

"What in thunder is this?" roared Grumpy, as he came to his feet in a huff. By now Stone looked as ruffled as he sounded.

"Take the stand," ordered Judge Whitlock, sternly.

"I object."

"Overruled, take the stand." The judge banged his gavel, leaning over as if to punctuate his command.

Captain Jordan swore Stone in. Grumpy trembled with anger. The judge reminded him sternly he had agreed to court rules and he was under oath.

Duffy read the bill again. " 'Merry Christmas to you and your son, Mrs. Scott. Santa Claus came in this morning and paid your bill in full.' Now is that your signature, Mr. Stone?"

"Hollyhan," said Stone painfully, "you know what that means."

"Just answer the question, Mr. Stone," demanded Duffy.

"Yes, that is my signature."

"When you received that pie, Mr. Stone, what did the tag on it say?"

Stone just sat silent.

"You are under oath; answer the question," demanded the judge.

"It said 'Merry Christmas.' "

"What else?"

" 'Thank you for a wonderful job.' "

"There was more," prompted Duffy.

" 'Be sure Santa Claus gets half of the pie,' " said Stone softly.

"Say that a little louder."

"It said, 'Be sure Santa Claus gets half of the pie,' " repeated Stone, very agitated, but loudly.

Snickers and muffled laughter rose from the crowd.

"Was the pie as delicious as you expected?"

"It was."

"Did you eat all of it, Mr. Stone?"

"I did."

"Well, now, Mr. Stone," chided Duffy, "even you recognized the elf in yourself. You do understand about Santa Claus after all, don't you?" He smiled smugly at Stone for a moment, then began to chuckle.

The judge pounded and pounded for silence as the crowd reacted. Despite his efforts to appear detached and unemotional, he shook with inner laughter at Grumpy Stone's helpless and hopeless plight.

"Thank you, Mr. Stone. You have been a most helpful witness," said Duffy smiling. "I have no further questions."

"Do you have any questions for the witness, Mr. Stone?" asked the judge with restored dignity.

"No, I guess not," said Stone sheepishly. "The Prosecution rests."

"The Defense rests."

"Mr. Stone," said Judge Whitlock, "would you please summarize now?"

George Stone was silent for a moment, collected himself, and thoughtfully approached the jury. No longer the confident bully, a bit wilted and humbled, he was still the professional.

"Gentlemen, despite the emotion and sentimentality

we have seen and heard, not one piece of solid evidence has been presented to you to guarantee the existence of Santa Claus. He is not here, and you and I know why that is impossible. Truth is your duty. The fact remains that Santa Claus is not real. You can find no other verdict. Thank you."

"Thank you, Mr. Stone," said the judge. "Mr. Hollyhan, will you summarize now, please?"

Duffy stood before the jury a moment, thoughtfully turning the Elf's Cap in his hands. "Gentlemen, every great faith is based on the belief that human beings are blessed with a potential that sets them apart from other creatures. As Christians we believe that difference is the Holy Spirit within each of us. Santa Claus is a manifestation of that spirit, of the unselfish loving goodness with which we were created. Expressing that divine gift through Santa Claus is to bring one's life into full bloom. It is one opportunity for us to be one with God. Every Christmas is a revival. Old Santa is there providing a beginning for children to understand the gift of Christ, and the opportunity for adults to participate in a truly Holy experience."

Duffy paused to survey the faces of the jurors. "I would like to think that we have convinced you that psychologically, philosophically, and theologically we need Santa Claus. If he did not exist, the Master would need to create someone to take his place."

For a moment, he studied the Elf's Cap in his hand. "All the evidence you need is your faith and the understanding we have made known to you today. With that in your mind, please look deep into your hearts. Look for the elf in yourself in making your decision. Thank you."

Duffy ceremoniously put on the Elf's Cap and returned to his seat.

"Gentlemen of the Jury," said Judge Whitlock, "you have heard the arguments pro and con, and now you must decide the answer to the question, 'Is Santa Claus real?' I trust you appreciate the impact of your decision, so approach your verdict with prayer and care. Captain Watt has offered you the use of the cabin on the good ship, Elissa. Constable Burke, will you see that the jury is not disturbed?"

"Yes, Your Honor."

"Gentlemen, when you have a decision, ring the ship's bell three times three and I will call this court to order ten minutes thereafter to hear your verdict." He punctuated his order with a resounding bang of his gavel.

Judge Whitlock and Grumpy Stone came over to Duffy's table. With wrinkled brow, George Stone was obviously in deep thought.

"Any regrets, Gentlemen?" asked the judge.

Smiling, Duffy shook his head.

"You better believe I have regrets," complained Stone bitterly, "but I can't blame anyone but myself. I don't understand you, Hollyhan. I took you for a bumpkin and charged you like a bull, only to find you played with me like a matador."

"Stone, you made a lot of mistakes today. That is not like you," commented Judge Whitlock. "You underestimated Hollyhan badly. You took a negative position on a subject as controversial, if not holy, as Santa Claus. You were too sure of yourself and lost your temper."

"Yeah, Hollyhan set a trap for me and I dove into it head first."

"Surprise can be a defensive weapon," added Duffy.

"Want to speculate on the verdict?" asked the judge.

"I would wager we get no verdict," said Stone. "That jury is varied enough they will never agree on a Yes-or-No verdict."

"Well," mused Duffy, smiling confidently. "I'll bet you a steak dinner for the three of us tonight that we do get a verdict."

"You're on," said Stone quickly.

"You see, Stone, no one told them their verdict had to be a simple yes or no. If they paid attention, and I believe some of them did, I gave them an honest, truthful and safe verdict."

"You're bragging," chided Stone.

"We'll see." Duffy laughed. "I supposed by now you would realize this is my briar-patch and I know these people better than you do. That is one more mistake you made today."

"You're the slick one, Duffy," said Grumpy. "I get a case now and then where your approach would be effective. Are you interested in the big money?"

"That is a flattering and generous offer, George. I was in the big money back east for years, but I came to realize all you truly get out of life is a living. I wanted to slow down and enjoy it. I decided time is worth more than riches. Life here is relaxed and easy. The people are friendly and interesting. Money won't buy more than that."

"Well now, that explains things. You're not the amateur after all," said Stone.

"You see, my father was a judge, and I grew up in and around his court. I learned both love and law from some of the best."

"I wish I had been aware of your past," moaned Stone.

"Some cases are fought on pure law and fact. Now that is your briar-patch, and I would hesitate to challenge you there. The question today involved no law, so it could be debated in terms of emotions, customs, morals, sentiment, love and faith. The trick is to recognize the difference."

"Duffy, it looks like the only satisfaction I can find in this event is that I exposed you as a fox with long ears who only acts like a rabbit," laughed Stone.

"Yeah, you did that. I'll have trouble avoiding some business now. But I can find some satisfaction in exposing you, too, George. People will know that old 'Thunder-and Lightning' Stone is really just an old elf in wolf's clothing."

"I would also like to think that I found a friend, Duffy, and I admit that I don't deserve it," said Stone seriously. "I sure owe you some apologies."

"I'll be pleased and proud to be your friend. Please don't change your style because of today's event. You see, I admire and respect your brand of strict logic and law. It is professionals like you that keep this nation together. We all depend on you. We need you."

"Those are kind words, Duffy, and I thank you for them. I must admit that you and your witnesses said things today that made me think of Santa quite differently. I see the old elf in a new light now."

"Bless you, George, and may your Christmases be all the merrier for it."

"Gentlemen," said Judge Whitlock, "you two have made this old man happy and proud today. I am privileged to know both of you."

"Here, here," responded Duffy.

"It has indeed been an experience," laughed Stone. "I won't soon forget this day."

Elissa's bell rang loudly three times three. Excited voices and scurrying people signaled the eagerness for the jury's decision.

The judge looked at his watch, "Ten minutes, Gentlemen: Let's see who buys the steaks."

Soon everyone had returned to hear the verdict.

Bam, bam, bam pounded the judge. "This court is now in session."

"Mr. English," said the judge. "Are you getting all these events properly recorded?"

"Oh, yes, Sir. This is fantastic."

"I think some folks will want copies, Mr. English," said the judge.

"Just read it all in the *News*. Right, Mr. Jenkins?"

"Right, Tommy," responded the editor.

The judge turned to the jury, "Gentlemen, do you have a verdict?"

"Yes, Your Honor, we do," said the foreman, confidently.

The judge looked at Duffy and smiled, then at Stone and raised his eyebrows. "Would you read the verdict, please?"

The foreman stood, cleared his throat and read loudly and proudly, "We, the Jury, unanimously agree that Santa Claus is as real as Uncle Sam, and that is as real as you and I."

The crowd burst into cheers and laughter. People came to Duffy to shake his hand and congratulate him. Judge Whitlock just sat quietly, smiling and filling his pipe, as he watched the merriment.

Suddenly the crowd became quiet, and many began to gather around Grumpy Stone. For once he was frightened and at a loss for words.

Dave Jenkins' voice broke the spell. "George, I believe I am most qualified to put into words what these folks are thinking about you right now. We witnessed an exciting event today, and we enjoyed every minute of it. What's more, we learned much about Santa Claus and ourselves. We also gained considerable insight into your character, and you have captured our admiration. You lost this argument today, George, but like it or not, you also won a lot of friends. You see, we know we need your kind of professionalism as frequently as we need Hollyhan's. We would like to shake your hand as understanding friends and wish you a Merry Christmas."

Grumpy's distress melted away into the warm handshakes and winning smiles from the crowd of admirers around him.

"A Christmas steak should be medium well, don't you think, Your Honor?" Duffy chuckled.

"Yes, Duffy, and with mushrooms, onions, and a sprig of holly," said the judge as he laughed.

"Indeed!" said Duffy. "And how do you want your crow, Mr. Stone?"

"Hrrumph!" grumbled Stone.

"I must return this cap and bell to the kids," said Duffy, as he put on the Elf's Cap, and danced around shaking his head, ringing the tiny bell.

Judge Whitlock began to laugh. "What a clown you are, Duffy."

"Duffy," shouted Stone, "you're a Christmas leprechaun."

Duffy and Judge Whitlock began to laugh louder and louder until even Grumpy Stone started to laugh.

Soon the three of them were walking together on The Strand. Duffy was playing his guitar and singing, "I believe in Santa Claus."

Judge Whitlock and Grumpy Stone, arm in arm, were shouting, "Merry Christmas" to everyone. They began to sing with Duffy and motioned to others to join. The Strand and doorways and windows filled with waving and singing people.

Justice had been served and faith preserved. The sun was shining again in Galveston.

A Dave Jenkins' editorial in the Galveston Daily News *proposed an "Elf's Night on the Strand" to celebrate the joy of Christmas and the great revelation about Santa Claus. Costumed people of every heritage danced and sang their native Christmas songs. There were fiddles and hornpipes, colored lamps and carolers, Christmas greetings and laughter, sugar plum vendors and clowns. All who loved Jesus and believed in Santa Claus wore Elf's Caps with jingle bells on the topknots. From this beginning, believers spread the seasonal custom of an "Elf's Night on the Town" across the nation.*

The winds and fortunes of time seemed unkind to old Galveston. The Strand's place in the sun was slowly fading away. But the love of a few has renewed the spirit in so many. Today, The Strand is reviving and becoming a place for us to relive and enjoy much of the best of our heritage.

Out of the dim light of the past on the wings of fond memories and loving care appears a tall ship, Elissa, gleaming in the sun, lofty and proud. She has returned to rekindle the legend she helped to begin and spread its memory across the land. In season, there atop the foremast, she too wears an Elf's Cap, and rests content at her moorings as the angels smile again on old Galveston.

Notes on
THE ELF'S CAP

"The Elf's Cap" is set in historic Galveston, Texas, and includes many authentic details. Truly, Galveston was the first cosmopolitan city in Texas. The famous commercial street, The Strand, faces on the waterfront in several places. From the port of Galveston and the commercial establishments on The Strand, people and commerce flowed into the infant Texas. Most of the original buildings exist today. Many of these are preserved to maintain the atmosphere of Galveston in the late 19th Century. The historical Strand area offers a delightful visit to natives and tourists alike.

The barque, the Elissa, was indeed in port in December, 1883, with Captain Henry Watt, its owner and master, as in the story. Elissa, beautifully restored by the citizens of Galveston, is once again moored and sails from Pier 21, where so much Texas history began. Its present site is near the scene of the happenings in "The Elf's Cap." Significantly, December, 1982, saw an elf's cap atop the Elissa's foremast as related in the story.

The *Galveston Daily News* served most of Texas as well as the city of Galveston at that time, and is the oldest newspaper in continuous operation in the state. The editor was David Jenkins. With the exception of Captain Watt and Dave Jenkins, all the characters are fictional.

The Garten Verein existed then and still serves Galveston as a civic and community center. The Palmetto House was a restaurant and hotel in Galveston in the 1800's. The Morgan Shipping Line operated from Central Wharf near Pier 21, carrying passengers and freight.

Much of Galveston is a time capsule, being preserved for enjoyment today and many tomorrows. "The Elf's Cap" was created to become part of that heritage.

The Charge of the Elf's Brigade

The little Texas frontier town bustled with activity. Families from the outlying ranches waited to complete their Christmas shopping. Horses and wagons lined the streets, and anxious people filled the stores. A brisk dry wind out of the northwest had swept the skies clear and bright. The air had the feel of Christmas, but with the freight wagons from Galveston eleven days overdue, the faces of the people didn't reflect happiness.

Sounds of a galloping horse echoed up the street as a rider hurried into town. As he approached the livery stable, he yanked off his hat. Waving it excitedly, he shouted, "They're coming, they're coming! I can see them from the ridge."

Cheers and elation rose from the impatient merchants and waiting customers as they rushed into the street. Slowly, a string of heavily loaded freight wagons rolled into town. Eager hands quickly carried the boxes, crates and barrels into the stores. The gloom gone, everyone was smiling again—everyone except John Slade.

John was busy loading a wagon behind his store. As he placed a sack of flour into the front of the wagon, he saw his driver hobbling into the alley on crutches.

"What's the matter, Tom?" he called.

"A horse at the livery stable kicked my leg, Mr. Slade. Doc says I can't walk on it for a week."

"I'm sorry to hear that, Tom. Is it bad?"

"Doc says it ain't broke, but right now it sure feels that way. Mr. Slade, I know how badly you need me right now. Those supplies are more'n a week late. The men at the Lucky Star Mine are out of food, and it's only two days to Christmas."

John Slade stood silent for a moment, thinking. "I must find someone to deliver these supplies now, Tom."

Together they went into the store. John Slade took his hat off the rack. As he untied his apron he spied Tooter Callihan admiring a small saddle in the back of the store. He stopped short, flashed a little smile and eased over to slap Tooter on the back.

"I've noticed you admiring the saddle before, Tooter. Are you thinking of buying it?"

"Yes, Sir," replied Tooter. "It would make a fine Christmas present for my son, just his size. But I can't afford it this year." Tooter hung his head despondently.

"I know you're proud of Billy. He is a fine boy. Say! I have a rush job that needs doing right now. It would just about pay for that saddle. Are you interested?"

Tooter almost jumped with excitement. "Am I? You know I am, that is, if I can handle it."

"Thought so," replied Mr. Slade. "I know you can do it, Tooter."

"What is the job, Mr. Slade?"

"I have a wagon load of supplies out back; it's mostly groceries. Since the supply wagons just got into town, I'm a week late delivering it to the Lucky Star Mine. You know those men are hungry, and it's Christmas. Tom there got kicked on the leg, so I need a driver."

Tooter took off his hat slowly, thinking. He whopped his dusty jeans with his hat and exclaimed, "Sure I can do that, Mr. Slade. Let's see, tomorrow is Christmas Eve. If I leave right away, I'll get there before dark. I'll come back first thing in the morning."

"I'll have that saddle wrapped up and waiting for you, Tooter."

"That would be great!" said Tooter, wide-eyed with excitement. "Molly is at the dress shop. I'll go tell her about the job and get my coat out of the buckboard. I'll be ready to go in a few minutes."

"I'll have a canteen and some lunch in the wagon by the time you get back."

Tooter rushed out of the store and up the street almost dancing with glee. Five minutes later he climbed onto John Slade's wagon.

"Here is your lunch, Tooter, and the canteen is under the seat," said Mr. Slade. "I've found a box for the saddle. I'll wrap it with burlap and put a big red ribbon on top."

"Wonderful! but don't you tell Billy now, ya hear."

"I promise, Tooter, I promise." said John Slade, with a smile and a wink.

"Giddap, now," shouted Tooter as he slapped the reins on the horses' backs.

Tooter headed south out of town and, a while later, turned onto the wagon trail that crossed the rocky flats toward the Lucky Star. The thought of surprising Billy

with the little saddle made him so happy he had to do something. He tried singing. That wasn't very good, so he tried whistling. That wasn't much better. Suddenly, he remembered the harmonica in his coat pocket. Quickly he retrieved it and started playing "Jingle Bells" with great gusto.

Two men appeared out of a clump of cactus. They stood in the trail waving their arms for Tooter to stop.

"Now, what is this?" said Tooter, as he reined his wagon and team to a stop. One man stood in front of the team while the other approached Tooter, pulled his pistol, and said, "This is a holdup, Mister. We need those supplies."

Tooter's heart sank.

The robber kept his pistol pointing at the shocked and frightened Tooter as he put his foot on the wheel hub and started climbing onto the wagon. Halfway up, the robber's foot slipped off and he fell to the ground with a thud. His pistol flew into the rocks and fired. The startled horses bolted, knocking the other robber to the ground.

Tooter nearly fell off the seat, but he saw his chance to escape.

Quickly he hazed his charging team in a circle, scattering sand and rocks onto the confused robbers. In a moment, he was racing back toward town.

"Giddap—giddap," he yelled.

The robbers collected themselves and ran for their horses. Tooter had a good start, but the loaded wagon was no match for the horsemen. Moments later the robbers caught up to Tooter.

"Go, go!" he shouted to the team.

One of the robbers fired a shot. It ripped into the sack of flour in the front of the wagon. Flour began to pour out into the front wheel causing a sudden thick white cloud behind the wagon. The robbers couldn't see. Thick cactus and boulders kept them in the narrow trail. They had to fall back.

Wide-eyed with fright, Tooter used the moment's advantage to think. He kicked the sack of flour to keep up the protective cloud while he searched for something else to foil his pursuers. Looking back into the wagon, he spied a large tin of black pepper. Just what I need, he thought. He bounded crazily on the wagon seat as he leaned back to reach the pepper. He managed to get in three more kicks to the sack of flour and two whoops at his horses. He held the pepper between his knees while he tied the reins to the wagon seat.

"Follow the trail, hosses, follow the trail," he yelled.

Frantically, he placed the pepper under his arm, kicked the flour sack again and dug into his pocket for his knife. By the time he had pried the lid off the tin of pepper, the sack of flour was empty. He retrieved the reins with one hand while he held onto the pepper with the other. The white cloud began to clear, and soon the robbers caught up again.

Just as the riders drew close to the wagon, Tooter

poured the pepper onto the wagon wheel. A small cloud of pepper blew up behind the wagon. The robbers' horses began to snort and buck. Tooter looked back in time to see both riders fly through the air and land tail first in a cactus patch.

Tooter tried to laugh and shout at his horses at the same time. The robbers tried to scream "Ouch" and sneeze at the same time. This comical wreck upset the race in Tooter's favor.

Back in town, Tooter reported his adventure to all who would listen. Riots of laughter arose and people marveled at his lucky and clever escape. For others, it wasn't all a laughing matter.

"What can we do, Sheriff?" asked John Slade.

The sheriff, too, was more worried than amused. He scratched his head and frowned. "That was only part of a big gang of rustlers and thieves that escaped across the border last summer. Now they are sneaking back again. The trees, tall cactus, and rocks in the flats are a good place for them to hide. I'll wager they're camped out near the creek."

"They are desperate for food and supplies," said John. "If you leave town with a posse, they may come here."

"That is what worries me," said the sheriff. "There are so many of them, and this is such a small town. All I can do is send for the cavalry."

"That will take two weeks or more," said Tooter.

"I will send word to the fort for help right away. That's all I can do," said the sheriff. "I'll keep some men to guard the town."

"Mr. Slade," said Tooter, "I still want that saddle. I've been thinking, with a string of pack horses, I can probably make it. I could follow the old Indian trails up along the ridges and stay out of sight until I get beyond the flats."

"Tooter, you have already earned that saddle. How can I ask you to do more?"

"Mr. Slade, I can't go home now and leave those miners hungry. It's Christmas."

"Thank you, Tooter," said John Slade, looking worried and thoughtful. "If you do this, I'll add a blanket and bridle to the saddle."

"That's great," shouted Tooter. "It's a deal. I'll be here with the horses when the moon rises. I want to be out of town and out of sight before sunrise. Then too, tomorrow is Christmas Eve. I want to get back here for that saddle and the rest of the outfit for Billy."

"Tooter, if you believe you can do it, then I know you can. It's late. Get some rest now and I'll get the supplies out of the wagon and ready to load on the pack horses."

At midnight, Tooter was packed and riding out of town. Sunup found him high on the ridges working his way along the old Indian trails. The heavy packs and string of horses made the going much slower than he had expected. It was late afternoon when he reached the Lucky Star Mine. Cheering and grateful miners helped Tooter unload his horses quickly so that he could hurry back to town.

Tooter reached the edge of the flats just after sundown, his horses too tired to continue. He couldn't try the high trails in the dark, and the moon wouldn't rise until after midnight. He found a secluded spot away from the trail and reluctantly made camp for the night. He would not be home with that wonderful little saddle for Christmas morning. With a heavy heart and a tired body, he tried to sleep.

He dozed restlessly for a few hours, then got up to check on his horses. Here and there among the boulders and cactus in the flats he could make out the glow of many campfires. There were more by the creek. The sheriff was right, he thought. It is a big bunch of outlaws.

In the stillness of the night he could hear an owl hoot across the flats, then another answer beyond the creek.

Such a beautiful, but sad night for me, he thought.

He tried to rest and managed a short snooze. Strange sounds from the trail toward the mine awakened him. He could not make them out. Rifle in hand, he went to investigate. Creeping cautiously along the trail in the grey gloom of starlight, he rounded a boulder and came face to face with a pair of reindeer.

Only then did he recognize Santa's voice urging the tired little team on. "What's the matter now, Dancer?" called Santa. "Something up there?"

"It's me," answered Tooter.

"That doesn't sound like Dancer. Who is ME?" asked Santa.

"Tooter Callihan!" came the surprised reply.

"Tooter! What are you doing out here? It's Christmas. You should be home with Molly and Billy."

By now Tooter had rushed around to the heavily loaded sleigh, "Shhh-shhh," he cautioned. "The flats out there are full of outlaws who would steal all this in a flash."

Santa sat down in dismay. "Oh, my!" he groaned. "My reindeer are too tired to fly, already I'm late, now this. How do I get to the other side, Tooter? Please help me."

"I'm trapped here too, Santa. I can't get home in time for Billy to get his saddle for Christmas. I could go around by the Indian trails in the morning, but that won't help either of us tonight."

"It's Jesus' Birthday, Tooter," said Santa. "He forgets no one and neither can I. I can't wait. We must do something now. Think, Tooter, think."

"It sure looks impossible," said Tooter, shaking his head in despair.

Tooter leaned on the sleigh, staring blankly at the bags of toys. His eyes focused on a brass bugle in one of the bags. An idea began to form.

"Hearing is believing. If I can make them believe—," he thought aloud. "Sounds, yeah, the right sounds."

He reached for the bugle. "Santa, do you have any firecrackers?"

"Yes, a big bag there for the party over at the orphans' home."

"I have a plan. It's wild, but it will work. I know it will. Listen! We'll run that whole bunch of outlaws clear out of the state."

"How?" asked Santa.

"We'll use their ears and their imaginations."

"How?"

"We'll sound enough like troops of cavalry to scare 'em right out of their underwear," said Tooter, excitedly.

"How?" asked Santa, again.

"By shouting and galloping my pack horses around and around over that patch of smooth rock over there to sound like troopers passing by. Then, we'll set off firecrackers, and I'll blow 'charge' on that bugle, and race across the flats to town."

"Say, you did get that name 'Tooter' when you were a bugler in the cavalry, didn't you?"

"Yep. Now let's get ready," answered Tooter.

"Could you deliver some of these toys and things around town for me, Tooter, so I can get back on schedule?"

"Yep, I'll get my horses, but remember, no noise until we are loaded."

"Yep," replied Santa, smiling.

Tooter saddled his horses while Santa prepared bags of toys and lists. Quickly they filled the huge pockets of the pack saddles with Santa's toys and gifts.

"Now, I need a little moonlight, Santa. The moon will begin to peep over the ridge most anytime now."

Tooter filled his pockets with strings of firecrackers and tied the bugle onto his saddle pommel. "I believe I'm ready, Santa."

"No, not yet. You will need this, Tooter," said Santa, as he handed Tooter his elf's cap. "Put this on and I'll put your hat in one of the packs."

"Well, look at me," said Tooter, as he put on Santa's cap. "Does this make me an elf?"

"Yep, you are an elf until the job is done tonight. I hope it is a pleasant memory," said Santa, with a twinkle in his eye. "It's Christmas. I have faith the Lord will see you through."

"Yep."

"Here comes the moon. How do we begin?" asked Santa.

"We need noise. Let's shout just anything so they will hear voices. When we see some of their campfires going out, we'll know they are alarmed and listening?"

"Okay, then what?"

"Then, I'll gallop my horses a few rounds. When I light this cigar, I'll start some firecrackers and begin the bugle calls. That is when both of us should be on our way."

Santa nodded.

"Are you ready?" shouted Tooter, at the top of his voice.

"I'm ready," called Santa.

"Start hollering," yelled Tooter.

"Ho-ho-ho," shouted Santa. He followed by singing "Jingle Bells" as loud as he could.

Tooter yelled everything that popped into his mind and changed his voice with each yell to sound like troopers. "Whaaa-whooo. Giddap, whoa, move over. Outta my way, dummy. Who put the overalls in Mrs. Murphy's chowder? You dirty dog. Oh, do-da-day. Merry Christmas. Mary had a little lamb. Hello, Sergeant. I like Grandma's cookies."

Santa was laughing at Tooter's silly yells and trying to shout something useful too, "Down the chimney. Up the chimney. Tooodle-oo and chipmunks, too."

Tooter stopped his shouts and held up his hand a moment. "Some of the fires are going out, Santa. They hear us now."

"Yes, I see."

"Let's go, Santa," said Tooter.

"Merry Christmas," replied Santa. "I'm ready."

Tooter galloped his horses in a small circle passing over the smooth rocks again and again. The clattering hooves of the shod horses sounded like groups of troopers passing the same spot. As the sound of the galloping horses pierced the still night air, the flats quickly became a beehive of excited activity.

Everywhere, sleepy outlaws stumbled to their feet, putting out their fires and listening intently to the unexpected sounds.

Tooter stopped and lit his cigar. He waved again to Santa as he lit a string of firecrackers and tossed them among some rocks. Across the flats, the explosions echoed like shots from troopers' carbines and sent the awakened outlaws dashing for their clothes and horses. The surprise had only begun.

Tooter lit another string of firecrackers and reached for the bugle. Halfway through "Charge", the firecrackers began to pop. Out on the flats, the outlaws' alarm turned instantly into wild, abandoned fright.

Rustlers and thieves rushed about, collided, stumbled and fell in their frantic rush to avoid the imagined troopers and save their very lives. Shortly, riders in every stage of dress darted among the rocks and cactus in a frenzied effort to find a way to escape the dreaded cavalry charge.

Boldly, Tooter led his string of toy-laden pack horses at a gallop on the wagon trail straight across the flats toward town. Between lighting strings of firecrackers from his cigar, he would blow another charge. Here and there, shadowy riders dashed among the rocks, crashing into one another or a cactus now and then.

Angry shouts, frightened moans, and the snorts and pounding hooves of leaping, plunging horses evidenced the pandemonium reigning in the pale moonlight. Lost hats, boots, blankets and shirts littered the trail or hung about on thorny cactus limbs.

In an open patch of silvery moonlight, Tooter saw an outlaw rushing madly to escape. He was a picture of panic in his red flannels. He held his hat in his teeth and his pants in his hand. His pistol hung around his neck, but no shirt was in sight. Eyes wide, arms flapping, he appeared but an instant and scurried away into the shadows of the night.

Tooter was scared himself, but the ridiculous sight of the fleeing outlaw sent him into a fit of laughter. This was more than he expected from his daring charade.

"No one will ever believe this," he thought aloud. "I will need some proof if this wild tale is to be told."

He stopped long enough to gather two hats, three odd boots, one gun and a few odds and ends of clothes. Having tied these up in someone's nightsirt, he hurried on his way.

As the sheriff and his men guarded the little town, they heard all the noise and anxiously awaited the expected troopers.

"Holy Cow!" exclaimed the sheriff, as only Tooter and his pack horses appeared out of the night. "Where is the cavalry?"

"I'm all there is," replied Tooter, laughing.

Tooter explained his and Santa's plight, and how the sounds they made struck terror in the outlaws' hearts. As he told of the fleeting shadows, the shrieks and groans among the cactus and boulders, the men began to laugh. The picture he described of the rider in red underwear caused many to snicker with glee. And when he emptied the contents of the outlaw's nightshirt on the ground, the guffaws rose to a roar.

Relieved, the sheriff and his men knew the outlaws would flee across the border again, and, for Christmas, as least, the town and ranches would be safe.

"Tooter," said the sheriff, "in the last hour, you have done a job that would have taken a brigade of cavalry to do in the daylight. Now, we can all spend Christmas with our families, and we'll celebrate the memory of your ride again and again."

"Thanks, Sheriff," said Tooter. "I was mighty scared, but still it was fun. Will you and your men deliver Santa's toys?"

The men responded eagerly. Quickly each one took a

pack horse. In the pack saddles, they found lists, toys and elf's caps.

"Tooter, you need a rest," said the sheriff. "Go over to my office and get a cup of coffee while we get this toy delivery organized."

As Tooter left, the sheriff called his men together. "We owe Tooter something. He saved this Christmas for us and our families."

They all agreed and quickly formed a plan. John Slade hurried down the street to tend to it.

With happy shouts and ho, ho, ho's, the sheriff's men with the pack horses rushed off in every direction.

Tooter came out of the sheriff's office with his coffee. "Where is my horse?" he asked.

"John Slade took him over to the livery stable for a quick feed and some water. He'll be back shortly. Finish your coffee."

"Thanks, Sheriff, I will," said Tooter.

Presently, John Slade returned, leading Tooter's horse and a pinto pony sporting the new saddle, blanket and bridle.

"What—what is this?" exclaimed Tooter.

"You did so much for all of us, Tooter, we chipped in and added the pony for Billy."

"Oh-h-h-h, my goodness!" admired Tooter. "What can I say?"

"Well," mused the sheriff, "you might tell Billy we think he has a fantastic father."

"This is our way of saying thanks to you," said Mr. Slade. "Now, it's a long ride out to your ranch. You better get going."

"I can't remember being so scared, so tired, and so happy all in one night," said Tooter, as he climbed on his horse. "This is a Merry Christmas, isn't it?"

A while later, in dawn's first light, Tooter was almost home. He dug into his pocket for his harmonica.

Molly Callihan hadn't slept a wink. Her face reflected the night's loneliness and worry. She opened the door to peer at the sunrise.

"What's the matter, Mommy?" asked Billy, rubbing the sleep from his eyes.

Before she could think of an answer, they heard Tooter begin playing "Jingle Bells" with all his might. Moments later Billy climbed on his pony and Tooter held Molly in his arms.

"Daddy, Daddy, where did you get the pony and saddle?" squealed Billy in delight. "Look, look, Mommy! Daddy brought me a bugle, too."

Her face wet with happy tears, Molly smiled at Tooter. "Yes, Tooter," she said, "there must be a story to tell."

"Yep."

The next year the little town celebrated the memory of Tooter's heroic Christmas caper. The sound of firecrackers and a bugle preceded a stampede of comical riders in various states of dress charging frantically about the scene. Following these came the famous "rider in red" racing wildly into of town. Then Tooter rode in, wearing his elf's cap and leading a pack horse loaded with good things to share with the children.

This tall Texas tale soon spread across the land to create a lasting American custom. "The Charge of the Elf's Brigade" is celebrated annually by all who love to remember our Western heritage and Christmas tradition.

Wheee-Whooo the Whistle

This Christmas Eve in San Antonio had been pleasant, and the evening unusually warm. Wisps of silky fog appeared here and there in the dimly lit railyard. The little old steam engine, pulling only a tender and caboose, backed slowly onto its special display siding. It was proudly maintained there in honor of the men and machines that moved a nation into its destined place. An elderly engineer, a man from railroading's glorious past, climbed out of the cab and stepped gingerly over to throw the final switch. Another old engineer waited in the cab, closing valves to extinguish the rumbling flames in the little engine's boiler.

Herman poked his head out of the cab. "Need any help there, Leo?"

"Naw," came the reply, "when I need help throwing a switch our railroading days will be over."

Leo climbed back into the cab and looked at his watch, "Almost midnight, Herman."

"Yeah," said Herman, "sure enjoyed carrying those kids around town today. We had as much fun as they did riding in the caboose, blowing the whistle and ringing the bell. I wish Christmas and July Fourth came around more often."

"Uh, huh! Salty is a fine old engine. Wish I could run it to the coast again sometime."

"Sure, it's been there a thousand times in its day, but once more just for old times would be fun."

"Well, the big diesels do pull more cars."

"Yeah, but Salty could keep up with most of 'em."

"Not with much of a load, Leo."

"It's old and retired like us, Herman, but it's a proud old hoss and people love the memory of its working days."

"Hey, what time is it?"

"Less than a minute to Christmas. Get ready. Now!"

Herman blew the whistle long and loud. Old Salty announced to all who could hear it was Christmas Day at last. Leo merrily rang the bell.

As the sounds faded away a gentle stillness crept over the railyard and all San Antonio.

Leo took off his cap and looked up reverently, "Happy Birthday, Lord. Thank you for letting us share in the fun of Your Celebration. And, Lord, if You are of a mind, we'd sure like to be around to help again next year. Amen."

"Amen," said Herman.

They climbed out of the cab and started toward the station house.

"Hey, look at those patches of fog," said Leo. "That is about all the white we ever see at Christmas down here."

"Yeah! but that is enough for me."

When they reached the station house, they chatted about the day's fun while Jake pulled the levers to complete his switching. Just as they were turning out the lights someone banged loudly on the door.

"Hello in there," shouted an unfamiliar voice.

Jake, Herman and Leo were startled. They expected no one. The railyard was closed for Christmas.

"Who can that be?" asked Jake.

The banging on the door began again, this time firmly, perhaps desperately.

"Please, is anyone there?" begged the anxious voice.

Jake unlocked the door as quickly as he could. When he opened it there stood Santa Claus with soot on his clothes and little drops of sweat running through the chimney dust on his nose.

"Oh, I'm glad you're here," sighed Santa, breathlessly. "I need help."

In a chorus the three old railroaders answered, "Sure Santa, how can we help?"

"I'm late. This warm weather and heavy load of toys is exhausting my reindeer. I need the fastest diesel you have to help me with my run to the coast at Port Lavaca. Quickly now."

"But, Santa," pleaded Jake, "we're shut down for Christmas. There isn't a diesel engine or anyone to run it."

"There must be an engine. I heard its whistle. That is why I came here for help." He paused a moment as he remembered, "Oh, my! I forgot. Diesels don't whistle, do they?"

Leo and Herman looked at one another, wide-eyed, both heads nodded in agreement. "Salty can do it," they shouted in unison.

A look of disbelief flashed in Jake's eyes as he and

Santa turned to face the excited old engineers.

"It's oiled and ready," assured Leo.

"And the boiler is hot," replied Herman. "We'll be ready in a flash."

"It's too late, it's too late," chided Jake. "Salty can't make that run by dawn."

Leo and Herman thought a moment. "I believe Salty can do it," said Leo.

"Me, too," said Herman. "It won't be easy, but we've got to try."

"This is ridiculous," shouted Jake.

"Hush up and set the track, Jake. We're going," demanded Leo.

"And hurry," said Herman.

Jake walked away shaking his head and grumbling, but began to pull the levers to line up Salty's siding with the mainline to the coast.

"Do you have a flatcar for my sleigh?" asked Santa.

Everyone froze. There was no flatcar and it would take an hour to get one.

"Only a caboose," said Leo sadly.

"There, I told you we couldn't do it," replied Jake. "I told you, I told you."

Old Herman snapped his fingers once, then twice, and danced a step or two. "Give us the toys, Santa, we'll deliver them."

"How? There are too many," complained Jake, looking disgusted. "Besides we don't know where all the kids live."

"We'll get the old folks to help us. They know every kid and who is home or at Granny's or Aunt Polly's for Christmas. They can do it 'cause they know more about everything and everybody. Think of the fun we'll have."

"No! No! No!" said Jake, "we can't wake up enough old folks this late at night to get it all done."

"Yes, we can" shouted Leo. "The dogs will do it for us."

Santa couldn't believe the men. This did seem foolish and he had urgent and serious problems. "Please," he pleaded, "this is Christmas. I don't have time for this silly argument."

"It's not silly, Santa," assured Leo. "Believe us, we can do it."

"How can I believe that?" asked Santa in despair. "What can you do to get dogs to wake up enough old folks?"

"Wheee-whooo the whistle," was the excited reply from the old engineers.

"Yes, I see," said Santa thoughtfully. "And will the old folks know what to do?"

"Indeed they will, Santa," said Herman. "They will remember Salty's whistle and the Christmas run we made back in '25. When they hear us they will come."

"Now I remember," replied old Santa. "Many people came here to San Antonio to shop and the tracks washed out. Late Christmas Eve Salty took them home, running fast and whistling all the way."

"Yeah," said Herman, laughing, "and it was the hounds that howled when they heard the screech in Salty's whistle far away and woke up folks to meet their families at the stations."

Jake walked in a little circle shaking his head in disbelief.

"Ho! ho! ho!" laughed Santa, as he danced a little jig. "It will work, I know it will. The Lord will help them understand."

"This will get you back on schedule, Santa," said

Herman.

"And the old folks will have a wonderful Christmas adventure they will never forget," said Leo.

Santa had a thoughtful look on his face. "Sure, sure," he mumbled, as a great idea came to him. "The old folks, the best help I can get anywhere, so why not everywhere? There is no elf like an old elf. Let's do it! Ho, ho, let's do it! Quickly now!"

Everyone began to move at once. Everyone, that is, except Jake. "We can't do it in time," he shouted. "It's too late, and old Salty ain't fast enough."

"Doggone it, Jake, you're a pessimist," complained Herman. "Listen to me, you grumpy old coot; with only a caboose old Salty is greased lightning. We can do it if you'll quit complaining and get moving."

"Oh, all right," sighed Jake. "I'll help with the toys, but I still don't think it will work. Meet you at the caboose, Santa."

"My turn on the switch, Leo. You get Salty's firebox going," said Herman.

The excited scurrying of the old men would make one wonder who was the elf. Santa handed toys and lists of kids to Jake who stored them in the caboose. All the while Santa was laughing and shouting orders. "Now you begin in Seguin. I have already been as far as McQueeney. Understand?"

The rumble of the fire in Salty's boiler grew louder and louder, and in a moment, Leo blew the whistle. "The Jingle Bell Express is ready to roll," he shouted. "All aboooooooard!"

"One last bag," shouted Santa, as he pulled a sack from under the seat in his sleigh. "Here are caps like mine, with jingle bells on the topknots, for each of you and all the old folks. That makes you my official helpers. Now hurry, hurry, you have to beat the sun to Port Lavaca. It is a race you must win."

Whooooosh-whooooosh, Salty began to move.

"God bless you and Merry Christmas," called Santa. "Now, on Dancer, on Prancer- - -"

As Salty moved out of the railyard and onto the main track, the three men folded their railroader's caps into their pockets and put on the elf's caps. Leo shook his head, causing the little bell to jingle. Herman began to laugh.

"There goes Santa, headed toward the valley," shouted Jake, from the caboose. He pointed up into the night sky.

Herman tried to toot "Jingle Bells" on the whistle. It was awful, but they didn't notice. They shouted and laughed anyway. After whistling for several crossings, Herman leaned out the window for a look ahead. "There is the creek, Leo, faster now."

The firebox flashed and roared. The clickety-clack of the rails grew faster and faster. Salty's headlight swept a clear track ahead. Even the fluffy wisps of fog had disappeared.

"Ten more pounds to full steam pressure," yelled Leo.

"We'll need it all to wheee-whooo the whistle," reminded Herman.

By now the poles beside the track seemed to whiz past the little engine. Leo leaned out for a better look ahead. "There is Randolph Field. I can see the tower. Go, Salty, go!"

They crossed the bridge over Cibolo Creek, then passed the water tower in the town. They sped on through Marion toward McQueeney.

Jake sorted the lists and bags of toys back in the

caboose. He wanted to be ready for the first stop in Seguin. Leo scratched his head in obvious thought.

"Who do you think we'll get at the first station, Herman?"

"Well, there's old Pop Fagan and the Hopkins and maybe Auntie Mems. They would know."

"You mean T. Ford Fagan?"

"Yeah."

"Zeke and Maw Hopkins, wasn't Zeke the depot agent there years ago?"

"That's right. I know he'll be there," said Herman. "Hey! We just crossed the Guadalupe River. It's time to call our help."

"We're up to full pressure, give her a toot, Herman."

Herman pulled hard on the whistle cord and it happened. The whistle started low whoo'n then broke into a screeching wheee and choked off to a short whooo.

"Sing to 'em, Salty, sing to 'em. Tell 'em we're coming," shouted Herman and blew it again.

Whooooo-wheee-whooooooo.

Herman and Leo danced around the engine cab like joyful elves.

Zeke Hopkins' old hound, Billy Blue, lay asleep on the front porch. One ear twitched just a little, then he opened one eye. He stretched out to relax himself some more when he heard it again. He sat up quickly and tilted his head to listen real good. At the next whistle he cut loose a howl that shook the house. Zeke sat up so quickly he fell out of bed. In a flash he was out in the yard, rifle in hand and nightshirt flapping.

"What 'cha got, Billy Blue, what 'cha got, Boy?"

As he stood looking and listening he heard the next whistle. "I'm dreaming," he yelled, but no one heard him because Billy Blue was telling the world about it, too.

"Wake up, Maw, wake up and listen," shouted Zeke.

Before Billy Blue could trigger another howl, Maw was screaming, "It's Salty, it's Salty."

By the time old Billy Blue ran out of breath on the next earthshaker, Maw was on the porch. "Santa ain't been here yet, Zeke," she shouted. "That must be why old Salty is running and calling. Somebody is wanting help and I can guess who."

"Let's go, Maw, we'll meet 'em at the station." Zeke turned to run for his boots and Maw tied on her bonnet. A thought struck Zeke in midflight. More help was needed and fast.

"Fagan would know," he thought aloud. He stopped at the porch and looked back. There silhouetted against the light from the rising moon stood Fagan's chimney. Zeke rested his rifle over the porch railing and took aim. "Just a whisker higher," he mumbled.

Ka-whoom.

Zeke was half in the door when he heard the shot twanng off the chimney. "I can still do it," he shouted. "Haw! Haw!"

Hopping back onto the porch, while pulling on his second boot, Zeke saw lights blink on at Fagan's house. Just then Salty whistled again and Billy Blue explained it loud and clear for anyone listening.

Maw whizzed across the porch and Zeke grabbed her hand. She stopped short. "Maw, let's take the Willys. It will be like old times."

"Yeah, Zeke, yeah," she sighed. "Let's do it like old times."

Moments later the old Willys Overland was rattling down the road to the station. As they passed Fagan's house, they heard his old Ford backfire twice and they started laughing. Each knew a great adventure had just begun.

Maw and Zeke had lights on at the depot when both Salty and Pop Fagan's Ford rolled to a stop.

Jake handed bags and lists to Zeke and Pop. He explained about the caps and all Santa's instructions. Herman hopped around the little engine oiling everything while Leo watched the gauges.

"Hey, Maw," shouted Leo. "Them flivvers are a sight for sore eyes. Ain't it fun, Maw, ain't it fun?"

"It is, Leo, it is. I never dreamed we would do something like this."

"Bless you, Maw, now don't split your girdle rushing around here tonight, ya hear?" Leo laughed.

"I'm safe, Leo, didn't have time to put on my girdle. You mind you don't singe your whiskers at the firebox."

"I'm safe, too, Maw, burned 'em all off years ago, haw! haw!"

"Ya'll stop to visit when you come back, ya hear?"

"Great, tell all the old folks to listen for our whistle and come to the station."

"We'll bring the party. Gotta go now, Leo."

Herman climbed into the cab as Jake, looking worried and grumbling to himself, signaled to roll again. Everyone shouted, "Merry Christmas" as old Salty began to move. In an instant Herman turned to Leo holding up two fingers. Leo held up three. Neither said a word or moved.

Pow, popped the old Ford.

Each one folded down one finger. In a moment, Pow-pow! then, silence.

"You lose," said Leo.

"Yeah," replied Herman, as he began laughing. "You always were better at that."

"Well, I know Fagan forgets to advance the spark when he is in a hurry. That always was good for three pops."

"Fagan and his Ford, both classics. May they last forever," sighed Herman.

Oooooooo-ga. Ah-oooooo-ga. The sounds of the old cars faded off into the sleeping town.

Salty gained speed rapidly. Jake sorted bags and lists for the next stop.

"Hey, Leo!" shouted Herman over the noise. "The old folks and the old cars made me think. I wager we'll see more old cars, even horses and buckboards and such before this night is over."

"You're right, it's just natural for folks to be sentimental this time of year. When they hear Salty's whistle, it's thinking of good old times that makes them understand and come a-running."

"I can see it now," said Herman laughing, "Uncle

Muley Mulligan riding a shiny mule. You reckon he can still ride?"

"If he ain't dead, he'll be riding a mule; you can count on it."

Salty ran with all its might again. Herman leaned out of the cab and held his elf's cap on with one hand while he pulled the whistle cord with the other. Whooo-wheeee-whooo.

"I can smell the oil fields. We oughta see some lights in Luling any time now, Leo."

"Do you recall that Luling was named for a China-man, Leo?"

"Yeah, he owned a famous restaurant there when the town began."

Whooooooo-wheeeee-whoooo.

"Felipe Castillo is an old railroader from our time. Doesn't he live on this side of town?" asked Leo.

"You're right, over there somewhere on a little hill. I don't see any light."

"The moon is up and full now. Should see it. There, that lump on the hill to the right, that's his house, but there is no light."

Whooooooo-wheeeeee-whooooo.

"Surely he has a dog," worried Herman.

"Does Felipe like tamales? Of course he has a dog," chided Leo.

Whooooooo-wheeee-whooo.

Whooooooo-wheeee-whooo.

Old Felipe jumped up and waved his arms. "Mama Mia," he shouted and raced for his britches and keys to the old red Dodge.

As he chugged down the hill, a turn in the road faced him toward the tracks. He saw Salty's light straight ahead. Felipe blinked his headlights twice.

Whoooo-whoooo, came the quick response.

Leo and Herman danced with joy. "It's him, it's him."

Felipe leaned over the steering wheel shouting, "Andele, andele," and blew the horn as though it would make the old car go faster.

"I see another light in town," shouted Leo, "and there, headlights, who could that be?"

"Don't know," said Herman, "but they seem to be heading for the station. We'll know in a minute."

Salty began to slow down for the station. Felipe soon passed them, whooping and waving. When he saw the elf's caps, he too knew what had to be done. He was waiting eagerly when they pulled up to the platform.

Just then a fine old Cadillac rolled to a stop. An elderly man jumped out and rushed up to help Jake and Felipe with the toys. A lady remained in the car.

"Don't know them," said Leo, as he climbed down, oil can in hand.

"I'm Herman. Who are you, Pretty Lady?" called Herman loudly.

"I'm Dolly Svensen, Herman. My husband, Pete there, came home on Salty that Christmas back in '25. He owned cotton gins along this line."

"Bless both of you for remembering, Miss Dolly. Merry Christmas. Say! We'll be back through here tomorrow; round up the old timers and we'll stop for a visit."

"Fine, let's make it a party."

"Come on, you're wasting time, Leo. Let's roll," shouted Jake, waving his arms up and down. "We're behind schedule. Go, go! This is already impossible you know."

Amid laughing and shouting, Salty rolled again. Whooooo-whooooooo.

"Go, Salty, go!" shouted Herman as the little engine was puffing and blowing to pick up speed.

They rushed on into the night, whistling up more grand and happy old people. At Waelder, there were the Schultzs in a shiny green Packard and Rufus Williams in an elegant old LaSalle. On they raced, with Jake minding his watch and scolding them on at every stop. "You'll be sorry you lost this race."

They whistled long and hard for Flatonia. Sancho Cisneros was the first to arrive in his old Studebaker. Close behind came Julius Mantini in a Model A Ford. Just as they began to load the bags of toys, a wagon and team came rumbling and rattling out of the night. Nighthawk Smith stopped his wagon and hit the ground running while Mandy held the reins.

"How did you get hitched up so quick, Nighthawk?" shouted Leo. "I can't believe this."

"We were going home after a hayride, Leo," said Nighthawk, laughing. "It surprised us when we heard Salty's whistle, but we shoah knew what to do."

"Indeed, and bless you," replied Herman. "We need just a few very special old folks to help tonight. Ya'll are some of the best."

Old Jake studied his watch and wagged his head in worry. "We won't make it, I told you this wouldn't work. We gotta hurry! Throw the switch for Moulton and Shiner, Leo."

Leo threw the switch and shouted, "Merry Christmas," as he climbed aboard. "We'll whistle you back here sometime tomorrow, so's we can git all the braggin' done. Okay, Sancho?"

"You're on," shouted Sancho, as his old Studebaker

rumbled to life.

Slipping on their elf's caps, the joyful oldtimers rushed away, tooting and shouting to get their delightful errand done.

"You take the whistle on this one, Leo," yelled Herman.

In sight of Moulton, Leo began to whistle. First one light, then another, and another popped on in the sleeping little town ahead. Headlights began to show and Leo and Herman cheered.

"Give 'em another whistle, Leo."

He pulled hard on the cord.

Whooo-ooo-oo was all he got.

"It won't whee," cried Leo, in horror and despair. He tried again.

Whooooo-ooo-oo-o.

Herman's face was white. Jake yelled from the caboose. They all knew something was wrong, bad wrong.

"Oh, no," cried Leo. "We forgot water. We're running out of water. We can't make enough steam."

"What dummies we are," moaned Herman. "In all this fun and excitement we forgot water."

Salty began slowing down.

"We won't even make it to town, Herman. We won't make it," groaned Leo, almost in tears.

Herman shouted back to an anxious Jake. "We're out of water, Jake."

"I told you so. I told you so, you bumpkins," shouted Jake. He dropped his arms and hung his head in despair.

Salty was coasting along slowly now. Car headlights were waiting at the depot, but old Salty wouldn't get there. Even if it did, there were no water tanks for steam engines anymore; diesels don't need water. They knew it was over, all over.

"Hello," came a voice as a buckboard came rattling along the moonlit road beside the track. "Hello there, what is the matter?"

"We're helping Santa," shouted Herman, "but we're out of water."

"Stop 'er at the windmill over yonder on the other side of the track, plenty of water in the pond," came the reply. "I'll be right back with buckets and some help." The old man whipped up the team and raced on into town, his nightcap and long nightshirt flapping in the wind. At every bump in the road, he bounced so high they could see the station lights between him and the buckboard seat. No matter, he whipped the reins and yelled at the horses to hurry.

"Sure hope he's wearing something under that nightshirt," said Leo.

"We'll never know," said Herman laughing.

"He'll know every time he sits down tomorrow," snickered Jake.

By the time Salty coasted to a stop at the windmill, the headlights were streaming out of town. Soon old cars full of old folks, with buckets and tubs, chugged around the pond of water by the windmill. Close behind came the buckboard. Leo and Herman climbed up on the engine and shouted and waved as they waited to pour the water into Salty's tank.

The magnificent old people were a sight to behold. There were tall ones and short ones, skinny ones and fat ones. Some wore the most comical nightclothes imaginable: pink and blue and white, even red long-handles. Many had on boots and hats or night caps, but no one noticed. They all waded into the pond, whooping and shouting, and toted water to Salty.

Two old men with a tub slipped back into the pond with a splash, but never lost their grip. They came up grim and made it to Salty before they fell down laughing.

Somewhere out on the pasture a horse and rider raced toward the pond. Right at the water's edge the horse stopped short and the old rider flew over his head, landing with a splash in mid-pond. He didn't say a word; just stood up and grabbed the handle of a bucket Grandma Svboda was holding and together they raced to the engine. On the way back both of them began laughing and fell into the pond. When they sat up to catch their breath, Grandma said, "Never saw you get off your horse like that, John."

"Well, ya'll looked like you needed some help in a hurry, so I got off the quickest way I could."

They both fell back laughing again.

Jake and old man Tuts put bags of toys in the wagon and the old cars, and passed around the elf's caps, while Herman and Leo and the happy crowd of old people filled Salty with the water it needed. It was an outrageous ruckus and a splendid Christmas adventure for some of God's greatest creations, good old folks.

"Hey, Herman," shouted Leo, breathlessly between buckets of water, "who is that old man dancing around like an overgrown monkey with Jake and the toys?"

"That is Bartholemew Tuts," replied Herman.

"Bartholemew?" quizzed Leo.

"Bart, for short, he always says," replied Herman, "ran a boarding house here years ago."

"Bart's Boarding House?"

"Yeah, that was it."

Leo stopped short, half through pouring a bucket of water. "That old rascal," he said. "He threw me and the Sullivan boys out of there one night forty years ago."

"Did you need throwing out, Leo?"

"It was cold outside, Herman. We had to sleep in a boxcar," complained Leo, with an injured expression on his face.

"What were you doing, Leo?" demanded Herman.

"Patrick plays the harmonica real good. Herman, he didn't have to throw us out for that."

"And Michael? You and Michael were just enjoying the music, is that it?"

"Well, not exactly; you see, Mike was teaching me an Irish jig, that's all."

"Bless your little old hearts," answered Herman, in mock sympathy. "Now jig up some water in that boiler before I throw you off this engine."

Leo poured in his bucketful. "Since old Bart came out to help tonight, maybe I should forgive him. You think I should, Herman?"

Herman poured the next bucket of water over Leo's head. "Salty's full, Leo, let's get rolling," he said, waving to everyone.

The happy and proud old folks laughed and cheered as Jake finished his instructions and shouted, "Booooooard."

"See ya'll at the station tomorrow. Be there, ya hear? Merry Christmas now," said Leo, as he opened the throttle.

Salty began to move. Whoosh-whoosh.

As Salty picked up speed, the old folks began moving out to deliver Santa's Christmas toys, their noisy elation uncontrollable.

Salty hurried on with all its might, whistling to dogs and those special old people who would know what to do. More lights blinked on in response to Salty's whistle in Shiner. The Barchak's in a 1930 Chevrolet and Dolph and Helen Schwartz in a '32 Buick met them at the depot.

Old Jake remained despondent. "It's impossible you know," he complained. "We'll run out of water again for sure. You idiots are gonna ruin this Christmas for a lot of kids."

Salty raced on toward Cuero, running faster than anyone could remember.

"Cuero is next, Leo, the turkey farming capital of the world," said Herman.

"Yep," replied Leo, "sure enjoyed the Turkey Trot Festival there this year."

"We're gaining time again, Leo, but we're almost an hour late. We can't stand another delay."

"Jake is right, Herman, we're going to need a water plug again in Victoria," said Leo. "We gotta think of something."

"The Fire Department could fill us up. Who there would understand?"

"Sam Patterson drove an old fire engine around town last July Fourth. I read about it in the paper. Old Sam looks after a fire station there now. His brother Joe was the conductor on Salty's famous Christmas run in '25," explained Leo.

"Good, but he will need to know we need water, can't tell him that with the whistle," said Herman holding his head and worrying.

"Well, you better start whistling now, I can see Cuero."

Whooooooo-wheeeee-whooooo.

Whoooooo, whooo, wheeeee-whooooo.

"No lights, Leo, do it again."

Whooooo-wheeeee-whooo, whoo, whee-whooo.

"There is one light, ho, ho, and another one way out there; now, there, see over there," exclaimed Leo.

Whooooo-wheeeee-whooo.

Whooooooooo-whooooo-wheee-whooo.

"Bless their old hearts, here they come," giggled Herman.

As Salty pulled up to the station, three old cars chugged to a stop. Cheering and waving old people rushed up to the caboose as Jake waved them to him.

Quickly the bags and lists and elf's caps were handed around as 'fun-fire' flashed in excited old eyes. The frolic paused a moment at the unmistakable popping of an old green tractor that rambled upon the scene.

"Turk-or-Two" Thompson climbed down, flashing a half-acre smile. "Me and Old Poppin-Johnny are rarin' to go. Gimme some baggage."

"Turk, you wonderful old goat," whooped Jake. "Here is your load of stuff."

"You still raisin' eleventeen million turkeys?" questioned Leo.

"Well-l-l, no-o-o, but you know I got a turk-or-two," drawled Thompson, as he climbed back onto the tractor and shoved the throttle full forward.

Big Jake and Aunt Sally O'Leary rattled to a stop in their fine old Chrysler to claim the last bag of toys.

Leo busied himself oiling the engine as Herman rang the bell to add to the happy commotion.

Up a street Herman spied an old lady in her nightgown, hobbling along, cane in hand, toward the station. He climbed down quickly and rushed over to meet her. "Ruby, Ruby Schneider," shouted Herman, as he reached out for her.

"Herman," she cried, and embraced him for support. "You're a welcome sight to see."

"You, too, Miss Ruby. Bless you, and Merry Christmas."

"You're helping Santa, ain't ya?" she said, nodding happily.

"Right," said Herman, strutting around tossing his head so the bell on his cap would jingle.

"Hank knew it the minute Rosco howled and we heard Salty's whistle," sighed Ruby breathlessly. "Hank is too weak to walk, but he is back there yelling his head off for you. Is there any way we can help?"

"Indeed! Oh, yes, indeed," said Herman as he placed his elf's cap on her head. "Get on the telephone, Miss Ruby, call old Sam Patterson at the fire station in Victoria, and tell him what is happening. Tell him we will need water for the engine or we won't make it to the coast. You understand?"

"I understand," she said, eyes sparkling.

"Tell Sam this is a race. We gotta reach the end of the line in Port Lavaca before the sun comes up and we're behind schedule." Herman pulled out his watch and looked at it, frowning. "Oh, my!" he exclaimed. "Help us, Miss Ruby, help us."

"I can do it, I can, I know I can."

Whoooo-whooo whistled Leo.

"Gotta go, Miss Ruby, hurry now. Hey! We'll stop on the way back, bring Hank and the others down to the depot, ya hear?"

"Yippeee," shouted Ruby as she tottered back toward her house.

Herman grabbed another cap from Jake as he rushed back to the engine.

Salty began to move.

The clicking of the wheels over joints in the rails, the swish and roar of the mighty little engine increased the glow in the hearts and gleam in the eyes of the old railroaders.

"You know," said Leo, snickering, "someone back there said, 'This night is more like it used to be than it ever was before.' "

"Haw! Haw!" laughed Herman. "That's right."

"How are we doing for time, Herman?"

Herman looked at his watch. "We're still gaining, perhaps only half an hour late now. If Sam is waiting for us, we might catch up."

"Victoria is in sight, Leo, let's call our help."

Whooooo-wheeee-whooo.

At the fire station, Sam Patterson hung up the phone, pulled on his boots and grabbed his fire hat and coat. He shook two young firemen awake. Two dalmatians sleeping by the stairs raised their heads to watch this strange activity. There had been no alarm, only a telephone call.

"Wake up, wake up, boys. I need some help, hurry now," said Sam.

"I don't hear any alarm," said Jimbo sleepily.

"Come on, Sam," complained Skip. "There is no fire or you'd be raising thunder, waking up the whole station."

"Listen, boys, listen to this old man. You've heard me tell of Salty, the little old steam engine that built this town, and its famous Christmas run from San Antonio."

"Yeah, Sam, that one and other tall tales," they replied sleepily.

"Well, Aunt Ruby Schneider just called from Cuero. Salty is running again tonight, helping Santa. It will need water at the station here. We gotta string a hose. Move now; we'll take the old engine."

"The Old Whopper-Stopper?" asked both firemen at once.

"Kee-e-rect," replied old Sam with an impish grin. "Hurry now."

Both boys sat on the sides of their bunks, pulling on their sox. "How much time do we have, Sam?" questioned Jimbo.

"About three minutes from the time the dogs start howling at Salty's whistle."

Already Speckles sat up, blinking, and Pepper tilted his head listening. In a moment, both dogs put up a fierce howl.

"Follow me! Boys, follow me!" yelled Sam, as he grabbed the pole and slid down to the engine room.

Both dogs raced down the stairs, barking and howling. Jimbo and Skip leaped up, rushing for their gear, and ran head on with a thud. Wide-awake now they dressed in a flash. By the time they slid down to the engine room, Sam was driving the old fire engine out the door. They ran after him and jumped onto the rear

platform. The race for the depot was on and they had to get there first.

The old fire engine churned on, lights flashing and bell ringing. The dalmatians on the seat barked and howled, and Sam leaned over the steering wheel into the wind. The tips of his long mustache tickled his ears as Jimbo and Skip laughed at the excited old fireman and cheered him on.

Whooooooo-wheeeeee-whoooo.

Whoooo-whooooo-wheeeee-whoooo.

Old cars chugged and wheezed as they made their way to the station. Running horses, rider's shouts, and rattling wagon wheels foretold the crowd gathering at the depot.

Sam slowed the fire truck as he wheeled by a fire hydrant. Jimbo jumped off with a hose end in his hand and Skip followed with a plug wrench. They connected to the fire plug quickly while Sam drove toward the depot. The fire hose peeled off the old fire truck in rapid flopping motions. A jiffy later old Sam stood majestically at the end of the platform, hose in hand, waving to Leo and Herman. "Stop 'er here," he shouted.

Salty rolled to an easy stop, and Herman helped insert the hose. Sam waved to Jimbo and Skip to turn on the water.

Jake was quickly surrounded by an eager and merry crowd of fine old people. There were bald heads, beards, mustaches, and bonnets, and hair curlers, too; but the glowing old faces reflected the ecstacy of the job they joyously came to do.

An old Hudson with big shiny headlights and a radiator cap that looked like a flagman with bright lights in his hands raced upon the scene. A big black man got out.

"Ace Watkins," shouted Leo. "You marvelous old rascal." Leo rushed up to shake his hand. "What is the railroad's best mechanic doing now-a-days?"

Ace pointed to a sign on the side of the old car. It read *Watkins' Garage.* "One of my sons has the touch, Leo. He runs our business now, and I rebuild old cars like this."

"You always were the best, Ace," said Leo.

"We still are the best," replied Ace, strutting in pride as he took the bag of toys and elf's cap from Jake.

Just then an elegant old Buick without a top chugged to a stop. A very properly dressed old chauffer opened the rear door for a well-dressed elderly lady. They walked, very dignified, into the little crowd around Jake and the toys. The merriment came to a sudden halt. Everyone stared at the very formal lady and her chauffer. Jake looked a long moment at both of them smiling.

"Clementine McDuff," he said bowing, "and Will Kelly." He grasped Will's hand in a firm shake. "I knew you would be here. I knew it. God bless both of you."

"I believe we can deliver a bag of those toys, Big

Jake," said Clementine, almost haughtily. She held out her gloved hand as if to demand it. Jake handed her two elf's caps and a large bag of toys. She put the bag at her feet and handed a cap to the chauffer. "Put that on," she said firmly, as she put one on herself. Looking about the silent crowd, a little smile slowly crept across her face.

In a sudden and surprising burst of emotion, she kissed Jake on the cheek. "Merry Christmas," she called. "It's our night to howl." She turned quick as a wink and raced gleefully for the old car. "Bring the bag, Williford," she said. "It's my turn to drive."

"Williford?" questioned Jake, snickering.

Old Will grimaced in despair, then grabbed the bag of toys and raced after Clementine. "Whaa whoo," he shouted, jumping with joy.

By now the spell was broken and the little crowd of old people began moving and chattering again.

As the old Buick sputtered to a start, Clementine put it in gear and shouted, "Last one through is a rotten egg."

A tall old gent rode into the happy crowd, riding bareback on a fat and sleek mule. "Gimme a bag, Jake," he shouted.

Jake handed him a bag, a list and a cap. "Never seen a mule with black rings around both eyes like that, Uncle Muley."

"Ain't he purdy?" replied Uncle Muley, proudly. "Best I ever had. Come on, 'Gator Joe, we got work to do. Eeeiii-ow."

Jake organized the delivery of toys until only one bag was left. A grand old man rode up horseback. His big hat, long mustache, tall boots, and a proud set in the saddle presented a picture from the past.

"Ah reckon that last bag is mine," he said solemnly.

Jake handed him an elf's cap and a list. The old man took off his big Texas hat and tucked it under the coil of rope on his saddle. Carefully, he put on the elf's cap. He still hadn't smiled; neither had Big Jake. The old man looked all around sorta slow like he was expecting something. He stuck a big hand out to Jake. "Gimme the loot, Jake," he said, dryly.

Jake handed him the bag of toys slowly as he too gazed all around as though he was looking for someone. He looked the old man right in the eye with his sternest face. "Yuh think yuh can git all of this thar in time, Dutch?" he asked.

"Can a coyotee howl?" asked the old man, as he tied the bag of toys to his saddle horn.

Jake winked back at him.

The old man leaned over toward Jake and pointed toward a little park. "See that smoke over yonder?"

"Yeah!" said Jake.

"Barbeque, you understand?"

"With beans?"

"How else?"

"Ummmmm," sighed Jake.

"Be ready when you get back, stop now ya hear?" drawled the old man. "We'll have the whole gang," he said, pointing to the old folks rushing away from the depot.

Jake just nodded.

The old man looked all around again and gently nudged his horse with his spurs, and slowly walked away. The old man turned and flashed a quick smile back at Jake, yanked off the elf's cap and slapped his horse on the rump with it, yelling, "Yee-Owww."

He was out of sight before Jake recovered from

exploding laughter. "Dutch Moller," he yelled, "you're the greatest."

"Water is in, time to go," shouted Herman.

Jake waved the men together as he looked at his watch, "These stops are taking too long," he sighed. "Three more stations to Port Lavaca, we can't do it before morning, we just can't do it," he said sadly.

"You're right, Jake," said Leo, wiping tears from his eyes. "You're right, we're out of time."

"We simply gotta do something," said Herman sniffling.

Old Sam listened sadly. "Look, look," he said. "Ha, ha, there come the Ross sisters on their bicycles. Ain't that a silly old sight. Hey! That gives me an ideee. Yeah! Yeah! Get 'em over here quick," he shouted.

Herman and Leo rushed to get the old ladies while Sam called his firemen. Jake just waved his arms and grumbled aloud. "Can't do it, can't do it," he cried. "Too late, can't do it."

Sam got everyone together and quickly explained. "Boys, you roll up the hose and take the old Whopper-Stopper back to the station. Ida Mae and Katy and I will go with Salty and get off with the toys and lists at Guadalupe, Decosta, and Placedo so Salty can race on to Port Lavaca. Okay?"

"Wha-a-a Whoo-o," shouted Leo. "That will do it, we can make it."

Leo and Herman rushed for the engine while Jake and Sam helped Ida Mae and Katy into the caboose.

"Get aboard," shouted Ida Mae.

"Time's awasting, let's roll," shouted Katy.

Whoosh, whoosh. Salty began to move again as Jake outfitted his new helpers with elf's caps, toys, and Santa's instructions. Only minutes later Leo whistled to the old folks at Guadalupe. Some lights were already on and others popped on as Salty's whistle called for help.

"Looks like Ruby is calling ahead, Leo" said Herman. "Bless her old heart. There is plenty of help now, and we're making up time." He looked at his watch. "Come on, Leo, let's hurry."

Groups of fine old people eagerly met Salty at Guadalupe, Decosta and Placedo. First Ida Mae, then Katy, and finally Sam got off with bags and lists, and Salty sped on to the coast. The spirit of the night's work was heightened by the nostalgia of the old cars, trucks, tractors, and horses. Everywhere plans were made for Salty's return.

Herman whistled long as Salty raced into Port Lavaca. Lights blinked here and there as understanding old people answered the call. As the old engine passed the gins and feed stores, a crowd was gathering at the depot at the end of the line.

Even Ora and Hez Paul had made it in from Clark Station.

Happy voices and glowing faces greeted Salty's crew as the engine pulled into the old station. Eager hands sorted the bags of toys and passed around the elf's caps.

The old people hurried off into the night to deliver Santa's toys, the three old railroaders stood quietly on the station platform looking east over the end of the tracks and the moonlit water of the bay.

"Well, I'll be a long-tailed monkey, we got here in time," sighed Jake. "We beat the sun, I just didn't believe old Salty could do it."

"Yeah," said Leo, "but I believed Salty could make it and we knew the old folks would do it, too."

"I'm as happy as I can remember," sighed Herman. "But I'm also tired and hungry."

"Me, too," said Leo, "but I never felt so good."

"Amen," replied Jake.

Near the end of the track, just beyond the depot, two firemen were dragging a hose. Another waved for Salty to move down to them. Quickly the old men complied.

As they climbed out of the cab, one of the firemen said to them, "Sam Patterson phoned from Placedo. Our fire station is right there." He pointed the way. "The coffee is hot, the sausage is cooking, and the pancakes are ready to pour on the griddle. Ya'll rest up now, we'll fill 'er up for your return trip. Oh! and Merry Christmas."

The three railroad men hurried away to the fire station for breakfast as the first hint of sunrise touched the skies above the waters of Lavaca Bay.

Returning to San Antonio, Salty wore an Elf's Cap. All along the line the old engine and all the old folks were Christmas heroes. They relived their night's adventures and the best of old times. Everyone agreed that in seasons to follow, Salty will visit before Christmas Day and the old folks will gather and parade and prepare for helping Santa Claus. After dark on Christmas Eve, old engines, fire trucks, old cars, riders and all their kin will ring their bells, whistle, toot and shout to celebrate Jesus' Birth and let Santa know they are ready to help deliver his gifts if needed.

Late that evening, Leo, Herman and Jake quietly parked Salty on its special siding in the railyard back in San Antonio.

As the rumble of the fire in Salty's boiler faded away, Jake reached a big hand out to Leo and the other to Herman. The old men formed a little circle.

"Lord," said Jake, "for us, the greatest gift of our lives is the experience we shared this Christmas run."

"Yes, Lord," said Leo, "perhaps we too gave the most we ever gave, just ourselves. Even now the joy of it seems to return a hundred fold."

"Thank you for the memories we now have to hold, Lord," said Herman. "The sparkling eyes and shining faces of those wonderful old people will light up our lives for years to come. We'll hear the harps of heaven in the sounds of their horses, wagons, tractors, and old cars, and such, and in the memory of their happy voices we'll hear the angels sing. Amen."

"Amen."

"Amen."

"Once more?" asked Herman, smiling.

"Yes, once," said Jake.

"Let's," added Leo, with an impish grin.

Whooooo-wheeeee-whoooo. The nostalgic echo of Salty's whistle made the old men's hearts swell with pride and joy once again. As the grand old sounds and the responding chorus of howling hounds gently faded away the stillness was broken again as the church bells of San Antonio began to ring. From every direction came crowds of people in the finery of the past to welcome Salty and its crew home. The mayor arrived in a vintage limousine to parade the old men through town and home.

New sounds and symbols have been added to America's Christmas scene. The steam engine's whistle, the fire engine's bell, old cars' horns, the rattle of wheels, and horses' hoofs, and the cheers and musical, loving laughter of old folks will add a cherished quality to seasons yet to come.

Notes on
WHEEE-WHOOO THE WHISTLE

The route of Salty's run is authentic. It begins in the Southern Pacific railyard in San Antonio. All the towns and landmarks mentioned are there, even the smell of the oil fields near Luling. Several picturesque old stations still exist along the line. In Port Lavaca, where Salty originated and got its name, the tracks end on the bayshore near the old station, looking east over the shimmering waters of Lavaca Bay. As in the story, the fire station is convenient to the track.

In the early days of Texas railroading, beginning long before the turn of the century, the little steam engine ran regularly between San Antonio and Port Lavaca. Such an engine, perhaps Salty, rests in a little park near the old station in Victoria today. Herman and Leo were indeed engineers from railroading's glorious past, and the old folks, though fictional, are a composit of grand old people as may still be found in this part of Texas.

Feathers and Bells

As Toby Miller rode up to his winter cabin in the West Texas high country, he noticed fresh tracks in the sand. "Wow! Biggest bear tracks I've ever seen," exclaimed Toby. "He came from the creek and left toward the mesa." The cabin door stood open, the broken latch lay on the ground. Toby saw the stable was wrecked and Sandy, his spare horse, gone. He gave Rosco a pat on the neck as he dismounted.

"We're in big trouble, Old Hoss," he said. "Wait here while I look around."

Toby pulled his rifle from its boot on the saddle and shucked a cartridge into the chamber. "I'll be more comfortable with this in my hand. That bear might decide to come back."

Rosco's ears stuck straight up; his wide eyes and twitching tail revealed his fear.

"Bet you can smell that bear, Rosco, take it easy now, it looks like he has been gone awhile," assured Toby.

Toby looked into the stable. The back rails of Sandy's stall had been knocked down from the inside.

"Looks like Sandy broke out himself. Hope he got out of here before the bear got in," he mumbled. "I don't see any blood."

Torn sacks of corn and the overturned water tub littered the shed. Not too bad, thought Toby, I can fix all this. The corn is okay, but I better check the cabin.

Inside the cabin, tables and chairs lay scattered about, but Toby's flour, beans, lard, bacon, and other food supplies seemed to be untouched. Toby looked all around as he straightened the furniture. This doesn't make any sense, he thought. There is nothing here to frighten that bear away. Why did he leave all this food? Toby stood scratching his head. Then he remembered his bucket of honey had been on the table.

"Rosco," yelled Toby, "that big polecat took my whole winter's supply of honey. I won't stand for that."

Toby rushed outside and mounted up. "Let's go find Sandy, then we'll get after that bear. I know bears, he will be back again in a few days. We gotta find him first or we'll all spend a hungry winter up here."

Toby followed Sandy's tracks off toward the creek. He spurred Rosco along at a lope for several hundred yards. Sandy's tracks looked closer together now. He must have stopped running about here, thought Toby.

"Whoa up, Rosco, let's listen a minute."

No creature, bird or insect made a sound.

"Something is around here, Rosco. It's too quiet. Let's hope it's Sandy." Toby whistled and shouted, "Sandy!"

Off in the brush a horse whinnied and Toby could hear him moving.

"Come here, Boy, that old bear is gone."

In a moment Sandy walked up and nudged both Rosco and Toby.

"Yeah, we're glad to see you too, Sandy. You were smart to break out of there. I learned a long time ago not to pen a horse up too tight. Those stall rails were easy for you to knock down, weren't they?"

Toby led Sandy back to the corral, fed and watered both horses. He fixed some food for himself and packed a bedroll and supplies for the bear hunt. He saddled Sandy, tied the cabin door shut and rode up the trail toward the mesa.

Carefully he followed the bear's trail, pausing occasionally to look and listen. Studying the trail signs he mumbled a rhyme to himself ———

> "Tracks and twigs, scents and sound
> Along one's path abound . . ."

Toby took a deep breath, "Sandy, I wouldn't mean that bear any harm if I thought he would leave us alone, but he smelled too much food in that cabin. I know he will come back. Let's get moving."

Toby enjoyed tending the cattle through the winter

up in the high country. Keeping the herd from scattering so they could be found in the spring was usually an easy job. One man was enough if he rode every day the weather would permit. Toby liked the long quiet rides and the campouts when he rode all the way to the river. He had two good horses and covered stalls for each. His cabin was warm and he had enough for all of them to last the winter. This left him long hours to study nature. He watched every living thing in the mountains and valleys. He knew every tree and bush, and the tracks and habits of every critter that walked or crawled. He could mimic the calls of birds and animals so well they often came almost close enough for him to touch.

Following the trail toward the mesa, Toby was trying to think like a bear.

Just before dark Toby found the bent-up lid from his honey bucket. "I bet he licked the outside of that bucket all along the way. About here Old Grizzly finally got it open."

In a motte of trees nearby Toby found signs that the bear had stopped to eat the honey. The grass and leaves showed the bear had sat on the ground and rolled on his back for some time.

"That big rascal sure had himself a good time, Sandy. I can just see him licking my honey out of the bucket. I bet he thinks he is the smartest bear in the mountains. Hey! Look, here's my honey bucket and it's licked clean as a whistle."

From the trees, the tracks led up a draw and toward the rough and rocky edge of the mesa. Toby stood thinking, with the empty bucket in his hand. He looked up toward the big green mesa. "Too late in the day to follow that bear up there, Sandy. We'll camp here tonight and pick up the trail in the morning."

About midnight Toby awakened to gusts of wind and a sudden chill. A cold rain began to fall. He and Sandy shivered in a steady downpour for several hours. Before daylight it all blew over and the cold air moved in dry and clear. Toby worked at getting a fire started and spent some time drying out his gear. By midmorning he had Sandy saddled up again and moved off up the draw.

"Sandy, that rain washed out every track. We'll sure have to hunt to find that bear again," said Toby. "Now where would I go if I were a honey-fed bear?"

Early the next morning, and only a few miles from the cabin, Toby found the bear's trail along a small creek. Among the bear tracks he noticed moccasin tracks. Toby studied these carefully.

"Sandy, these are fresh, only two, maybe three hours old and there's just one Indian following that bear. Hey that's too much bear for one Indian, unless he has a rifle. Uh, oh! He doesn't, see he stopped here to study the tracks. I can make out the print of the notch and the string where he rested the bow on the ground. Let's hurry."

Toby mounted up and hurried along the creek trail. Half a mile down the creek Toby saw a cave on a small ledge just above the trail. Inside he found the great bear dead. Two arrows were deep in the bear's chest and there were knife wounds in his throat. The Indian was gone, but spots of blood led out of the cave. Toby could tell from the way they were smeared that the Indian was crawling. That Indian must be wounded, thought Toby, as he hurried to follow the blood.

A hundred yards farther along the creek Toby found the Indian. He lay still beside the running water. Blood oozed from a badly injured leg and from scratches and bruises on his arms. Breathing, but cold and unconscious, he did not respond to Toby's efforts to arouse him.

"Old Buddy, you must be some brave Indian to do what you did. But, you'll be glad if I set this leg while you can't feel it."

Toby tore up his spare shirt and put a tourniquet on the broken leg.

Toby pulled hard on the Indian's foot and realigned the bones to straighten the leg. He cleaned and bandaged the wounds, and tied splints on securely. He cut holes in his blanket, put it on the Indian for a poncho and tied it on close to hold his body heat.

"Sandy, hold still while I tie him in the saddle and I'll lead you out of here."

Toby led Sandy at a fast walk. He didn't stop to eat or drink. Late in the afternoon they reached the cabin. Toby had to rest a few minutes to get the strength to take the Indian off the horse and into the cabin. He laid the Indian on a bunk and wrapped him in all the blankets and coats he had. As soon as he had a fire in the stove, Toby tended his horses for the night.

Back in the cabin he put a pot of water on to boil for treating the battered Indian, and another pot for bean soup. He chewed some jerky to renew his own strength. He rested a few minutes, then stepped outside to look around in the fading light of day.

Off toward the creek a big rabbit hopped out of the brush to feed on the short green grass in an open spot. Toby quietly eased back into the cabin and got his rifle. The sound of the shot faded away as it seemed to run down the creek toward the river miles away.

"Well, my Indian friend," said Toby, "and I hope

you are a friendly Indian, my plans for bean soup just changed to a rabbit stew." Toby cleaned and cut up the meat and put it into the stewpot with potatoes, salt, and a little garlic. He lit his lamp and added wood to the stove.

He tore up the rest of his shirt and tossed it into the other pot of boiling water. A few minutes later he fished out several large pieces of the cloth with a stick, hung them above the stove to dry, then removed the boiling water from the stove so it would cool.

With the cabin warm, Toby uncovered the Indian and prepared to treat his wounds. He removed the splints and bandages carefully. "The bleeding has stopped nicely, Big Fellow, now you just stay still while I clean this leg, put on fresh bandages, and install the splints again."

The Indian breathed regularly and seemed to be warm, but he remained unconscious. Toby cleaned the broken leg and the bruises on his shoulders and arms. The sterile bandages were dry; these Toby applied to the wound on the Indian's leg and replaced the splints.

"That is all I can do now, my friend, except wait for Mother Nature to rebuild your strength and put you together again."

Toby stirred the stew and moved it to the back of the stove, where it would cook slowly. Already the aroma was filling the cabin. He put a blanket over the Indian and laid down on his own bunk.

"Lord, I sure need your help to make all this right again. Please help me heal this Indian and send him home to his own. Amen."

Exhausted, Toby dropped off to sleep. Each time the fire in the stove died down, the cabin would begin to get cold. This would wake Toby. He built up the fire, checked on his patient and his stew, and went back to sleep again. At daylight Toby got up, tended his horses and fixed himself some breakfast. He had a jar of jam to sweeten his pancakes, but he couldn't forget about the honey.

"Old Bear, you sure have caused me a lot of trouble. I ain't so sure about this Indian problem, but I have a good axe and I know where there are some bee trees. So, I reckon I'll get me some more honey."

Toby heard the Indian take a deep breath and moan. He rushed over to check on him. His patient hadn't moved his arms or legs, but his face muscles moved slightly.

"Won't be long, Big Fella. You will be awake and feeling all your hurts shortly, I'll get ready."

Toby quickly put the cabin in order, got a cup of water, a pan for wet cloths, and stirred the stew. The Indian moved again. Toby pulled a chair up beside his bed and wrung out a cold wet rag. When he wiped it across the Indian's face, the Indian caught his breath and slowly opened his eyes. For a long moment he looked at Toby, then he tried to move and the look in his eyes changed to one of shock and fright. He tried again to sit up quickly, but half-way up his strength gave way and he fell back, gasping for breath. Toby wiped the Indian's face again with the wet cloth and spoke softly.

"Easy, easy now, you have enough trouble and I mean you no harm."

The soft tone of Toby's voice and the gentle wiping of the Indian's face slowly relaxed him. Toby smiled and put his finger to his lips.

"Shhh, be still, and I'll prop you up so you can figure all this out."

Toby rolled up his coat, his slicker and a blanket. He worked his hand in under the Indian's shoulder, slowly raised him half-way up, then shoved the roll under his neck and shoulders. As Toby eased him back down the Indian tried to move his arms. Suddenly his whole body went rigid and he held his breath.

Toby moaned in sympathy. "I can almost feel you hurt, Old Buddy. Better relax, you only make it worse."

The Indian relaxed and rolled his eyes in obvious despair. Toby removed the blanket from the Indian and pointed to the splinted leg. A frown formed on the Indian's face. Toby covered him again and offered him the cup of water. Slowly the Indian raised one arm, took the cup and drank. Toby refilled the cup twice more, then gathered a handful of small sticks from among the firewood. He pulled a string from the end of the blanket. Selecting a large dry stick he whittled on it until it roughly resembled a man's leg. While the Indian watched, Toby broke the stick and pointed to the Indian's leg. The Indian nodded in understanding. Next Toby went through the motions of pulling out on the foot, lining up the broken ends and easing them back together until they fit.

Again the Indian nodded in understanding. Toby put a small cloth on the break like a bandage, then put small sticks alongside like splints and wrapped and tied them in place with the string. The Indian smiled and nodded.

"Okay, Big Fellow, you know where you are hurt and how I fixed it; now who are you?"

Toby pointed to himself and said, "Toby." Then he pointed to the Indian.

"Mato," said the Indian. "Mah-toh."

Toby repeated the pointings, saying, "Toby, Mato."

The Indian nodded and smiled.

"Okay, Mato, let's try some food."

Toby filled two bowls with stew and put spoons in each. He sat down by Mato and gave him a bowl of stew. Mato watched Toby eat for a minute or two then carefully took the spoon and began to eat the stew. When he emptied the bowl, Toby refilled it. This time Mato ate eagerly. When he finished, he smiled and said something Toby couldn't understand.

"I don't know what you said, but you were smiling and you don't look mean or scared, so I'll take it kindly."

Toby removed the roll from behind Mato's head and laid him down easy. One long breath and he slept.

"Sleeping is your best medicine, my friend. You'll be here awhile, so I better make some plans."

While Toby thought, he chopped firewood for the cabin. Mato would need it to keep the cabin warm while Toby tended the cattle. Somehow, I must talk to Mato, thought Toby. To make this work we'll need to understand each other. Slowly a plan began to take shape in Toby's head. He had a pencil and a pad of paper. By drawing pictures of many things to point to, he and Mato could both learn words until they could talk. While he cut and carried wood to the cabin, he thought about the simple drawings he would need.

Mato awoke once more late in the day. Toby gave him food and water again. Mato went back to sleep.

At breakfast the next morning Mato sat up by himself and ate pancakes with jam. With help from Toby, he learned to say "pancakes." In the afternoon Toby carefully lifted Mato's injured leg and helped him turn so he could sit on the side of the bunk. He tried to stand, but quickly sat down again. The pain was too

much for even an Indian brave. Toby shook his head.

"No! No! Mato, that will be many weeks away. I will make you some crutches in a few days, that will help."

Outside in the cold dry air everything was still and quiet. Toby stood in the door of the cabin enjoying the freshness and view. When he turned to look at Mato he could see the longing in his eyes. Toby picked up a chair and set it outside the cabin door. He went back and made signs of carrying Mato out to the chair. Mato smiled and nodded. Toby put Mato's arm around his neck, slipped one arm under Mato's knees, then the other around his waist and carefully picked him up. Once in the chair Mato's eyes sparkled, and he took deep breaths of the clear cold air. Toby understood his feeling.

As they looked out toward the mountains, a hawk circled quietly over the trees and brush in front of the cabin. Toby and Mato watched him silently a few moments. Toby called to the hawk as another hawk would do. The hawk answered and circled toward the cabin. Now Toby made squealing sounds like a rabbit caught by a hawk or coyote. The hawk flew in close, just over their heads. Toby stopped his call and waved his arms to send the hawk away.

"Old Hawk, I fooled you, didn't I?" laughed Toby.

Mato's eyes were fixed on Toby in surprise and admiration. He said something and began to laugh with Toby as he pointed to the fleeing hawk.

They sat quietly a minute or two, enjoying the cool and quiet. Mato raised his hand for silence and pointed into the brush beyond the end of the cabin. He puckered his lips and chirped the fighting call of the cock cardinal. The redbird hopped around the bush seeming to look in all directions for the challenger. Mato whistled again and immediately the redbird flew up on the cabin roof above Toby and Mato. More calls and sounds mimicking two cock cardinals fighting brought more birds. In a moment four bright red cardinals danced nervously on the hitching rail almost close enough to touch. Only then did Mato stop and wave them away. Toby laughed admiringly and clapped his hands. Mato raised his head high and sat a moment in stony-faced pride.

This started a game they played many times, with every bird and animal within hearing distance.

The days were spent with each teaching the other to speak his own language. As they learned to understand each other, they shared many stories of their lives in the mountains and forests.

Toby learned that Mato hunted the great bear because he had raided the Indians' village four times, destroying food and badly injuring an old man, a little girl and two horses. Like Toby, Mato knew the bear was a spoiled maverick and would raid the village again.

Toby made crutches for Mato. As his strength returned, they spent many hours outdoors practicing bird and animal calls.

Mato stayed at the cabin alone on days Toby tended the cattle. One day he made a small drum of rawhide and an empty keg. At night he taught Toby drum talk. As they became better friends Toby began to think how lonely it would be when Mato became well enough to go back to his village.

The weeks stretched into December. Mato knew nothing of Jesus and Christmas. This excited Toby who set about changing that. Mato had Toby retell the whole story many times until he understood about Jesus' Birth and the celebrations. Only then did Toby explain the Christmas tree and Santa Claus. This, too, required much retelling. The Christmas antics of old Santa and the children were especially amusing to Mato.

One day Toby returned with a thorn bush he had cut earlier in the season so the leaves would fall leaving it white and bare.

"This is my Christmas tree," he said, as he whittled its stem and stood it in a knot hole in the cabin table.

"It not green."

"Most are green," exclaimed Toby. "This is my way. I'll explain."

"Umph!"

"Like the symbols on your teepee, my Christmas tree will have symbols too."

"No paint symbols on sticker bush."

"You will see."

"Umph!"

Toby took a big jar out of the cupboard. "These are some of my symbols," he said as he poured the mixed gumdrops and jellybeans into a bowl.

"Dumb berries."

Toby laughed. "Sweet berries, try one."

Mato wouldn't taste it until Toby ate one.

"Ummmmmm, more!"

Toby moved the bowl away. "Later."

"Umph."

Toby began to put the candy onto the thorns on the bush.

"How symbols?"

Toby explained to Mato how the tree helped him remember about Jesus' life as well as his Birth. "The white stem and branches represent the purity of Jesus and the thorns the only crown He ever wore," he said. "The red candy is the blood He shed for us and the white the forgiveness that is ours if we believe and ask. The green is the promise of life after death and the blue represents the heavens where Christ waits for us," Toby continued. "Yellow is for the sun and God's love that makes and sustains life on the earth. Purple is a royal color that reminds me Jesus is the Prince of Peace and the King of Kings."

Mato listened and watched, saying little more than an occasional "UMPH!"

Toby removed a large round concho from a saddle bag. He polished the ring with the star in its center until its silver gleamed. This he fastened to the top of his little tree, explaining it represented the star over Bethlehem at Jesus' Birth. Leather straps with holes punched near the ends made loops to pull around polished coins.

These Toby attached to the tree, adding glitter and symbolizing the parable about the talents. Crosses made by tying small twigs together and carved fish provided additional symbols. Each day Toby added more. By Christmas the tree was complete and Mato knew much about Christmas and Jesus. He also developed a sweet tooth that fancied gumdrops and jellybeans.

On Christmas Day fresh snow covered the ground. The sun rose into a clear blue sky sending beams of pure gold to play upon the snow foretelling the glory of the beautiful day unfolding. Mato and Toby watched silently from the front of the cabin. Nature presented a gift of its purity packaged in the cold dry air and elegant silence of a brilliant mountain morning.

"Only God, the Great Spirit, could create such beauty as this," said Toby.

Mato nodded.

"Men only disturb the stillness, make tracks in the snow, and put smoke in the sky."

Mato looked long and quietly at Toby. A bond of understanding and friendship continued to grow between them. "You wise man, Toby. How we make better?"

"We can't. We just love all this and believe in the Great Spirit that put it here."

"Yes."

"The Great Spirit sent His Son to tell us how to live. Today we honor His Birthday. It is Christmas, Mato. This day is greater than all we see and enjoy out there. Knowing about Jesus makes us feel beautiful in our hearts, here, inside."

Mato looked thoughtfully at Toby a long moment and began nodding in agreement.

"Let's go inside and enjoy the rest of the candy on our tree."

"You tell me again of Christmas."

"Of course, my friend, I'll tell you again."

Mato was smiling.

After retelling the Christmas story and enjoying the tree, Toby gave Mato his spare pocket knife. Mato gave Toby his string of beads.

Later in the day Toby removed the splints from Mato's leg. The wounds were healed, and the leg was straight. Cautious steps led to more as strength and confidence returned.

In two weeks Mato's limp was gone and in another he could run. With his strength restored he made plans to leave.

One clear day Toby and Mato rode to Eagle Point. Mato explained his village was near the river farther down the valley. Toby's horses couldn't go down the steep and rocky trails into the valley so Mato would walk from there.

"Goodbye, my friend," said Toby. "May we meet again. There is much I will enjoy remembering. In every cardinal's call, eagle's cry and far-away hoot of an owl I will hear your voice and think of you, Mato."

"And I listen for you in the wind and look for your tracks in the snow. I have much to tell, and when I tell I will think of you, Toby, my friend."

Proud but lonely, Toby rode back toward his cabin. The riderless horse beside him had his spirit low. Here and there he paused to answer an owl or a coyote's howl. Soon he had a chorus of friends filling the emptiness in his heart.

Years later Toby again returned to the high country. He owned the ranch now and it was time to teach his oldest son, Ben, to tend their cattle on the winter pasture. They cleaned out, repaired and supplied the old cabin, and made friends with every living creature close enough to hear. Toby set up his "sticker bush" Christmas tree in the same old knot hole in the table. Ben enjoyed hearing the stories Toby had to tell about his Christmas adventures.

Late in December a blustery spell moved in with howling wind and heavy snow. For days Toby and Ben had to stay in the cabin.

"Ben, the cattle will turn their backs to this wind and drift to the South. If we don't drive them back, we won't find them in the spring. It will be a two-day ride."

"I'll pack food and blankets, Dad."

"We'll leave at daybreak if it's clear."

"I'll be ready."

All the next day they rode south searching for cattle. They found the last of the herd just at dark near Eagle Point. Toby and Ben set up their camp for the night. They would start the cattle drive back in the morning. It was very late when they finished their meal and spread their blankets.

"It's Christmas Eve, Dad."

"I know, Son. I wish we were at the cabin to enjoy our tree."

"We'll get back there tomorrow. Anyway, look at the sky. There is no moon yet so the stars are very bright. How much more beautiful could the night be?"

"You're right, Ben. It's so clear I believe I can reach out and get a handful of the Milky Way."

"And so quiet I strain to hear the stars. They must make some sound when they sparkle so brightly."

"Hey! I did bring some jellybeans and gumdrops. I'll get them from my saddle bag."

Just a munch or two and both tired cowboys dozed off to sleep.

Toby and Ben awakened at the sound of a snap and a moan just beyond a clump of bushes. Quickly they pulled on their boots and went to investigate. As they made their way through the brush, something in the dark backed right into Ben's arms. Surprised, he could not run so he let out a shout and held on to it with all his might.

"I've got it, Dad. It's fuzzy, it must be a bear," exclaimed Ben.

"I'm no bear, you bumpkin," came a startled reply. It wasn't Toby's voice.

"Hold on, Ben," yelled Toby. "I'll strike a match."

In a moment, the light of the match revealed it all.

"Holy Smoke, Ben, let go. It's Santa Claus."

Ben stood too startled to speak.

"Well, Toby and Ben Miller. I just left your cabin. What are you two doing out here?"

"Chasing stray cows. What are you doing down here?" said Toby.

"I stopped to rest a moment and wait for the moon

to rise and stuck my sleigh on that big rock."

"We heard something crack."

"I broke a branch there trying to pry it loose. It's stuck tight and I'm late, very late. Can you help?"

"Of course we can," said Ben.

The moon began to appear over the ridge as they struggled to free the loaded sleigh.

"Oh, no," moaned Santa. "Look at the fog in the valley. That will slow me more. There are seven children at the fork of the river below the falls. How will I ever get there?"

"Only an Indian would know the trails in that valley," said Ben.

"Yes, you're right," said Toby. "Santa, do you have a drum in the sleigh?"

"Of course I have a drum, there in the back of the sleigh. What good will that do?"

"Perhaps I can get an Indian friend to help."

Toby took the toy drum and rushed over to the rocky ledge overlooking the valley. He tightened the drum until he got just the right sound. He sat down with the drum between his knees and thought hard to remember the drum talk Mato had taught him.

"If he is there, Lord, help him listen and understand," muttered Toby.

He began to thump out a message on the little drum.

The tiny but true voice of the little drum carried clearly on the still cold air in the valley below. Toby waited and repeated his call again and again. He listened with all his might for a reply.

Down the river the serenity of the sleeping Indian village was disturbed by a small dog's whining and growling.

"My son, see what bothers your dog so he will be

quiet."

A sleepy Indian boy stumbled out to console the fretting puppy. He stood to listen, then ran quickly back.

"Father, Father! Far up the valley a drum with a strange voice calls your name."

Mato rushed outside to listen. "Quickly, Son, my drum."

Dum-dum-ditty-dum, called the small clear voice of the toy drum. Mato listened carefully as a grin began to form on his face.

"It's Toby, my friend Toby, of long ago. Hurry, Son, hurry, hand me my drum."

Dum-dum-ditty-dum, came Toby's call again.

The booming answer from Mato's drum woke everyone in the Indian village. Seconds later it fell upon the straining ears of Toby, Ben and Santa Claus high on Eagle Point.

"Whaa-whoo," shouted Toby. "He is there, and he heard my call."

Back and forth the drums talked, until Toby stood up to say, "Santa, my friend Mato will be here shortly to deliver your gifts in the valley. Now let's unload your sleigh quickly and lift if off the rock."

Soon the sleigh was free. While Toby and Ben reloaded the bags of toys, Santa filled a bag for Mato. Toby answered an owl hoot and explained, "He is here."

Mato appeared from the trail leading into the valley. Eagerly Toby and Mato greeted one another. Mato gave Toby a band of feathers he brought as a gift.

Santa and Mato eyed one another carefully. Each walked a little circle around the other as Toby introduced them. Santa cuffed Mato on the shoulder.

"You are as big and stong as Toby said you were," said Santa.

Mato reached out to feel of Santa's white whiskers. "And you look like a cock cardinal with thistle seeds in his mouth as Toby said you did."

"Oh! Ho! What is this, Toby?" exclaimed Santa as he looked askance at Toby.

"Well, you do," said Toby snickering.

"Yes, I suppose I do," said Santa. "I just don't recall being described that way before."

He began to chuckle, then burst into a fit of laughter. Toby and Ben began to laugh with Santa. Mato stood stony-faced, watching the foolish scene. Slowly a little smile crept upon his face.

After recovering, Toby introduced Ben, and Mato

told of his young son. Ben explained about the stuck sleigh and the children in the valley.

Mato was eager to be involved in the story he heard so long ago. Quickly Santa explained the delivery, took off his Elf's Cap with a tiny bell on the topknot and placed it on Mato's head.

Mato swelled with pride. "Such an honor to wear your bonnet," he said.

Santa placed Mato's band and feathers on his own head. "Such an honor for me, too, Mato. Ho, ho, wait 'til the elves see my feathers." He looked thoughtful a moment. "I'll add some jingle bells to the band so they will know I am me." He laughed. "Feathers and bells, now that is a new cap for an old elf."

Mato replied proudly, "Today, my village will have its first Christmas tree to honor the birth of the Great Spirit's Son. And my son will hear the story of Jesus and Santa Claus."

"Bless you," said Santa.

Mato became fascinated with the sound of the tiny bell. He danced and wagged his head to hear it tinkle. His eyes sparkled with joy and he began to laugh.

Quickly, Toby got the jar of jellybeans and gumdrops and gave them to Mato. "These are for your first tree."

Santa gave Mato the toy drum Toby had used to call to him. "This is for you to place under your tree for your son, Mato. Now, remember this, every year I bring gifts to those children who celebrate the birth of Jesus by having a Christmas tree, and who believe in me."

"My village will have such a great tree with symbols of our own and others Toby taught me," said Mato. "And on this Holy Night, our drums will call to you,

Santa Claus, to tell you we believe and our children await your visit. Also our drums will tell you the elders stand ready to help if you call on a drum as Toby did tonight. Just strike three again and again until you hear our reply and our chief or an elder will come to you."

"I promise," said Santa.

"We will do a love dance around our tree to honor the Great Spirit and His Son's Birthday, then we will be silent and listen for your call," said Mato.

"Then God's eyes will be upon all of you and so will mine," replied Santa, as he took more bells from the reindeers' harness and gave them to Mato.

Ben handed his hunting knife to Mato. "Take this to your son, Mato. Tell him I made it myself and that one day I would like to be his friend also."

Mato set down the bag and drum and held the knife admiringly. Great appreciation shown on his face. Placing his hand on Ben's shoulder, he said, "Already you are my friend, Ben. My son will be pleased and proud to be your friend."

"You must hurry now, Mato," said Toby.

"You have given me so much, Toby. I have given you so little."

"You came tonight when I called, Mato. Now you do this for me and Santa and those children down there. You have given of yourself. What more can I ask?" said Toby.

"There is no greater gift than one's effort with a good heart," said Santa.

Mato stood quiet a moment and nodded as understanding began to show on his face. With the bag of toys over his shoulder he moved toward the trail, turned one last time, waved and vanished into the trees and brush. The jingling of the little bell faded away into the still night.

"It's late, and I must go," said Santa. "Thanks, Toby and Ben. God bless you both."

In a flash Santa climbed onto his sleigh and dashed off to complete this night's errands. Toby and Ben found themselves again in the serene stillness of the beautiful and Holy Night.

"I'm proud of you, Ben," said Toby.

"Why, Dad?"

"I know how proud you were of that knife and how much work you put into it."

"Yes, Dad, but I believe I enjoyed owning it most when I gave it away tonight."

"It will mean much more to that little Indian boy than you or I will ever know. Not just because it is a fine knife, but because of when and how he received it."

"I could see all that in Mato's eyes when I handed him the knife. I'll never forget that moment, Dad."

"Ben, every father looks for those signs that tell him his son has become a man. You have given me many signs, but tonight was the greatest. I couldn't be more pleased."

"Thanks, Dad."

"You also learned one of the best kept secrets of Christmas."

"Oh?" asked Ben.

"Yes, you see giving in the right spirit can be a greater satisfaction than receiving. It takes real maturity and a good heart to understand that."

"I understand that now, Dad. This was an adventure I will never forget."

Ben and Toby returned to their bedrolls. Both lay looking up into the clear night sky. The sparkling stars presented a Christmas display of God's creations.

"Merry Christmas, Dad. The cabin would be nice right now, but I wouldn't trade this night's adventure or this heavenly view for anything I can think of."

"Yes, Ben. We didn't expect this, but still, it sure is a great Christmas. Oh! and Ben, I will enjoy helping you make another knife."

"Oh, I knew that too, Dad."

"Thanks, Ben."

There was a moment of silence.

"Ho, ho," chuckled Toby softly. " 'I've got it, Dad. It's fuzzy! It's a bear,' you said. Ho, ho, well---it wasn't."

" 'A cock cardinal with a beard of thistles.' Ho! ho! Good night, Dad."

"Good night, Ben."

The Great
Christmas Turnabout

For two days the Mystery drifted powerless, wave-tossed and wind-blown on the blue waters of the western Gulf of Mexico. Captain Ed and Jo-Jo had worked endless hours to repair the engine. At last, they returned to the wheelhouse to wipe away the sweat and grease, and try again to get the big shrimp boat under way.

"This has been a dickens of a fix, Cap'n Ed," said Jo-Jo. "It's late and I sure am tired. What day is it, anyway?"

"Oh, my," replied the captain. "I believe it's Christmas Eve. We've worked so long on the engine I lost track of time."

"Oooooo-weee! We should have been home last night, Cap'n. We're too far south to make it in time now."

"You're right. It looks like a lonesome Christmas for us this time. Let's see, I believe Brownsville is our closest port. We'll go in there for fuel and a rest, and return to Brazosport up the Intracoastal Canal tomorrow."

Captain Ed tried the starter again. This time the big diesel burst into life with a rumble and a roar. Mystery turned its bow toward the shore and began to run swiftly with the rolling sea. Hours later Mystery was made fast to the dock and its engine stilled at last.

"It sure is quiet. I believe everyone in Brownsville is asleep," said Jo-Jo.

"It's three o'clock in the morning, and it is Christmas day. Folks should be asleep."

"Yeah, sure. Hey! Merry Christmas, Cap'n."

"Merry Christmas, Jo-Jo."

Both men began to laugh. "Here we are dog-tired and 300 miles from home for Christmas. What's so merry about that?" asked Jo-Jo.

"Well, we are safe and sound. Let's be thankful for that."

"You're right, Cap'n. But we only caught about fifty pounds of shrimp. What shall I do with them?"

"Ice them down in a chest. They are the biggest and best I've seen this season. We'll take them home with us tomorrow."

"Okay."

"Let's get through cleaning up and get some sleep."

Just as they finished hosing the deck a voice from the shadows away from the dock called to them. "Hello there!"

"Hello yourself," replied the captain.

"I'm trying to find Pancho Diaz. His houseboat was here last year." The voice was closer now.

"I saw Pancho in Corpus Christi last week. His boat is there somewhere. Who wants to know?"

"I do," came the reply, as Santa Claus appeared in the light beside the Mystery.

Captain Ed and Jo-Jo were both speechless with surprise.

"Will you help?" asked Santa.

Finding his tongue, Captain Ed replied. "Of course we will, but how?"

"I have toys for the Diaz kids and seventeen others I have lost between here and the Florida Keys. They are the last of the children on my list. Their families are shrimpers and boatmen and move around a lot. There are patches of clouds and fog along the coast, and it is very late. I won't find them all without some help."

"We will help here, but you will need more help than that, Santa," said Jo-Jo. "Hey! I just called home from the telephone booth here on the dock. We can call friends in Corpus Christ, Port Lavaca, and Freeport. My brother is in Rockport, and I have uncles in Galveston and Port Arthur. I am sure we can find others, too."

"That's a good idea. It would be a great help," said Santa.

"The boatmen could deliver your gifts to lost children in their ports so you could hurry on around to the Keys," said the captain.

"Excellent," replied Santa, "but how will I find these helpers quickly this late at night?"

Jo-Jo put his finger on his forehead to signal his brain to go to work. "I know," he shouted as he rushed to the wheelhouse. "We'll ask them to go to their boats and turn their spotlights up like this as beacons, then blow their horns like this." Mystery's light reached to the wisps of clouds high above and the blast of its horn was loud as thunder.

"Wow! that will work," said Santa. "Ho, ho, let's do it. Quickly now." He turned to rush away.

"Wait! Wait!" called the captain, "First, let me see your list. Some of the children may have moved here."

"Oh! of course. It's on the seat in my sleigh over there in the parking lot."

"I'll get it," said Jo-Jo, as he hurried away into the dark. "Hot Dog, there is gonna be some fun in this Christmas yet," he shouted.

When he returned they took the list into the wheelhouse to study it in the bright light. As Cap'n Ed and Santa checked the list, Jo-Jo stood by, thinking. An idea popped into his head. He snapped his fingers, winked at Captain Ed and rushed below.

"Ah-ha, here is one," exclaimed the captain. "Jimmy's father has his boat on the ways over there for repairs. He'll be here; I can find him. Now this last one, Betty Sue; her father just bought the shrimp house near the end of this dock. Jo-Jo knows where she lives."

"Good, good," said Santa. "I'll get their toys." He returned shortly with the children's gifts and elf's caps for Jo-Jo and the captain. "Bless you both for being here when I needed you. Now call ahead quickly and get those beacons up. I'm on my way. Ho-ho-ho and Merry Christmas."

Jo-Jo and the captain laughed at the spry old elf as he rushed off into the shadows. They heard the jingle of the sleigh bells and his eager shouts as he raced on into the night. "You have a sly grin on your face, Jo-Jo. What have you done?"

"He-he, ho-ho," snickered Jo-Jo. "I slipped our chest of shrimp into the back of Santa's sleigh. He and his elves will have the makings of a tasty feast when he gets home."

"Hey! I like that," said the captain. He began to laugh. "We sure pulled a turnabout on old Santa and his crew tonight. Oh-ho! and we sent our very best. Hurry now, let's get to the phones."

"Let's pass the word, Cap'n Ed. Let's pass the word so others can help make it a bigger surprise."

"Why not? We'll make this a year for Santa and his elves to remember. Everyone has good things prepared for Christmas. If they sneak a bit of their best into Santa's sleigh, there will be a great southern feast at the North Pole this Christmas Day."

"By golly! Cap'n , this is fun. You know, this is going to be a really Merry Christmas after all."

Captain Ed and Jo-Jo spent the next hour calling boatmen they knew along the coast who in turn called others. Santa's run to the Keys was marked by waiting and willing helpers in every port. All used their spotlights and horns to signal to him and, as agreed, they slipped some of their very best into the sleigh for the surprise feast at the North Pole.

With the boatmen's help, Santa found all the lost children and returned to his home with the turnabout surprises smuggled aboard his sleigh. The elves were ecstatic; nothing like this had ever happened before.

The magnificent food made a glorious feast truly worthy of the season. The heaping helpings of savory southern cooking were beyond the normal capacity of Santa's crew of elves. There were shrimp and snapper, oysters and chowder, hush-puppies and gumbo, pralines and fried chicken, turkey and cornbread dressing, tamales and guacamole, biscuits with strawberry preserves, candied yams, hams, and Key lime pie, and more and more galore.

Dazzled by the luscious aroma and incredible goodness of southern dishes and desserts, the elves stuffed their little tummies and lavished much more than customary ecstasies over every morsel. Their rapture grew until one by one the elves removed their caps and became giddy. Slowly a glaze crept across their little eyes until all of them became totally mesmerized by the heavenly foods and nectars from the southland paradise.

By and by the elves were lounging about in the solid comfort of being elegantly fed and suspended in a perfect state of bliss. Even Old Santa relaxed and enjoyed the afterglow of superb southern hospitality.

Days went by and still the elves were pudd'n-headed and entranced. Santa began to worry.

Weeks went by and still the elves remained unconcerned. Santa was distressed. Nothing he said effected

any change in the attitude of his elves. There was work to be done. It was time to begin making wagons and dolls for next Christmas.

Months went by and still no work was begun. Everywhere Santa found elves in Texas hats, sombreros and boots while others were singing Cajun songs. Here and there groups in straw hats discussed cornpone and magnolia blossoms in slow southern drawls. When he came upon the baseball caps, sun lamps, flowery shirts and sunglasses, he broke into a galloping panic. All his words were useless. The elves were struck with awe-inspiring complacency. Everywhere their bags were packed, and now and then some of them would break out singing, "That's what I like about the South."

Santa's distress was now beyond measure. The cheerless prospect of the forthcoming Christmas without toys demanded immediate and drastic actions.

Santa appealed to the nations. He was promised subcommittee investigations of the elf problem within the decade. He needed help now. Everywhere he heard only of budgets, priorities, agendas, jurisdictions, restrictions, and over-worked bureaucrats and politicians.

In despair he went to the governors and was smothered again with anguished cries of regulations, budget deficits, jurisprudence, party platforms, subversions, bipartisan bamboozlement and porkbarrel gerrymandering, but he got nothing of substance to help him with the elf problem.

Santa was desperate. There was no work going on in his workshop. The growing calamity would soon be beyond repair. Something profound had to be done with all haste.

"What to do, what to do?" said Santa, as he worried out loud. "Dear God, please help me. I have appealed

to the highest authorities in the nations to no avail."
He sat down despondently, his face a picture of gloom
without dimension.

Presently, just a freckle of an idea began to creep
into his head. He raised one eyebrow as the thought
took root in his frazzled and tattered brain. He gave a
little snort and stood up quickly. Peering off into
emptiness for a second or three, he clapped his hands
together with a resounding whap and danced a little jig.

"Of course, Oh, Thank you, Lord," he shouted, "the
children. They are my most loyal supporters. I'll write
to the children."

Quick as a cricket he went to his desk and found
paper and pen. All day and all night he wrote letters,
letters and more letters to children all over the land.

The kids responded, eagerly. In class rooms, play-
rooms, at recess and at home, the situation was
addressed with the utmost gravity. As the worry spread,
a plan began to emerge. The children wrote letters by
the hundreds, then thousands and millions to presi-
dents, senators, mayors and clowns. The elf problem
became a grave national concern. However, not so
much as a squeak resounded from the great cogs and
wheels of government.

In desperation, the children found a greater inspira-
tion. They turned their attentions to the North Pole
and wrote directly to the elves. Their letters began to
arrive by two's then four's and bags and finally by the
truck load. Santa put all the letters in one huge pile
and called the elves together.

"These letters are for you," said Santa.

The elves were unmoved. Their little minds were still
all tangled up.

Santa was bewildered. "The children believe this

mess is intolerable," he chided. "They believe it is worse than the seven-year itch and eleven kinds of home-work," he pleaded.

Still there was no response from the elves. They remained mesmerized, moon-eyed, and content.

As Santa wagged his head in despair, he took a letter off the pile and opened it.

"This letter is from the Cub Scouts and Brownies. It says, 'We, the undersigned, promise to mind our parents if you elves will mind Santa Claus.' It is signed by pages and pages of wonderful children."

One or two elves began to pay attention and to walk slowly toward the great pile of letters.

Santa opened another letter, "This one is from a third grade class. It says, 'Dear Elves, We promise to write to you every year. When we hear jingle bells, it will remind us that we love Santa and all of you. If you leave the North Pole, we won't know where to send your letters.' "

More of the elves were responding now and the glaze was beginning to fade from their eyes. Others began to move toward the letters.

Santa opened another letter. "This one says, 'Dear Elves, Grandma will make us more cookies next Christmas if we promise to help. We promise. They are chocolate-coated, double-decker super whiz-bangers. We will send you some. Now please get to work, Love, Jimmy and Debbie.' "

All the misty glaze was gone from the elves' eyes. They were crowding around the marvelous pile of letters now. Some were beginning to pick up an envelope here and there. It was working. Like magic, the childrens' letters were working.

Quickly, Santa opened another letter. "This is from Miss Betty's Sunday School Class. It says, 'Dear Elves, God made kittens to purr and puppies to wag their tails, then he made elves to help Santa Claus. We love you.' It is signed by the whole class."

There was just a moment of silence, then a burst of excitement and motion as the elves rushed to the glorious pile of letters. The old spell was broken and a new one was well under way. Everywhere the elves were reading the children's letters. They snickered and hollered, laughed and cried. The letters were traded and read and reread until the elves were again as simple-hearted and loveable as they ever were before.

Bright and early the next morning, each elf tied a tiny jingle bell to the topknot of his cap to remind him constantly of his Faith and duty. They all put on their caps and merrily went to work. The messages of love in the children's letters had charmed the elves into being, once again, just themselves. Santa's workshops were beehives of activity and the elves were cheerful, whis-

tling and singing again. Santa's storehouse for toys began to fill and the children's miracle became a most celebrated affair.

At last, the governors took up the elf matter in official conclave. It was their studied opinion that while everyone relished southern food only southerners were totally immune to lingering hypnotic trances induced by the ecstasies of down-south cooking.

In their great wisdom, they unanimously passed the following resolution:

"Whereas, Southern Hospitality being totally boundless and uncontrollable, the elves are sure to be exposed again. It, therefore, becomes mandatory to effect some immediate and positive action to protect the elves and guarantee the Christmas expectations of future generations. Be it, therefore, resolved that the southern states pronounce Santa Claus and his elves honorary citizens, and thus, invulnerable to all forms of lingering trance caused by over-indulgence in Dixie delights."

The appropriate legislatures were swift and forthright in their compliance with the governors' resolutions. Santa Claus and all his elves received certified, irrevocable citizenship in all the southern states, territories and the Conch Republic.

Captain Ed, Jo-Jo, and boatmen everywhere vow to stay ready to repeat their night's work, whenever Santa needs them. The Mystery, now retired, rests in a place of honor to the men and boats who pioneered an industry and sparked a Christmas tradition. Every year Santa comes to visit Mystery and the children. After dark on Christmas Eve, Mystery turns its spotlight to the heavens above and blows its horn. Boats and boatmen who know and believe repeat its signals all along the coasts.

Southern Hospitality is as warm as the sun, tender as a smile and contagious as fleas, so the Christmas Feast at the North Pole and the children's loving letters continue year after year, keeping Santa and his elves jolly and fat.

In celebration of this great Yuletide adventure, the President declared the Elf's Cap with a jingle bell on the topknot to be a seasonal and national symbol of faith, love and peace, and an everlasting promise of a Merry Christmas for children everywhere.

Another Christmas Book
by
Zeno Zeplin

A Novel

SECRETS OF SILVER VALLEY

ABOUT THE AUTHOR

Zeno Zeplin, a native Texan has a B. S. degree from Texas A. & M. University and is retired from a professional career in Engineering and management. A lifelong interest in traveling and history and now his grandchildren inspired his writing Christmas stories to enhance the Faith with new activities and symbols born of the spirit, history and culture of the Southwest. He believes a nation as old, large and diverse as America should not be content with Christmas stories and traditions from only its Northeast and old England. He also believes our annually repeated repertoire of Christmas literature and customs contains too little reference to our Faith.

Zeplin's purpose is to entertain people of all ages with the Christmas reverence and revelry of the South and West. His captivating yarns present grand new images and joyful new activities to expand the dimensions of Christmas celebrations for Americans for generations.

His first five stories were combined in one book, *GREAT TEXAS CHRISTMAS LEGENDS*. A sixth story to present Hispanic Christmas traditions became the novella *SECRETS OF SILVER VALLEY*. These two books were first published as Official Sesquicentennial Commemoratives in 1985 at the request of the Texas Sesquicentennial Commission in Austin. They are now available in these hardbacks, illustrated by Zeplin's daughter, professional artist, Judy E. Jones.

Zeplin reports more books are in the works.